SWEET DECEIT

A SWEET COVE, MASSACHUSETTS

COZY MYSTERY

BOOK 4

J.A. WHITING

To hear about new books and book sales, please sign up for my mailing list at: www.jawhitingbooks.com

For my family, with love

CHAPTER 1

Angie Roseland rode her bicycle along the street that ran behind her Victorian mansion's property. She and her three sisters lived together in the eighteen-room house on a quiet, cozy street in the seaside town of Sweet Cove, Massachusetts. The late afternoon sky was a brilliant blue and the air was warm and clear. She pulled over in front of a small, light gray Colonial style house with a "For Sale" sign at the edge of the lawn.

A bit of the paint was peeling on the front and sides of the home and two shutters hung slightly askew. The front grass was overgrown with weeds. It made Angie sad to see the home in disrepair. Even though the house's property line butted up against her own tree-lined back yard, she didn't know anything about the people who used to live here.

The sound of a car's engine caused Angie to turn to see Betty Hayes, a successful Sweet Cove Realtor, bringing her car to a stop at the curb. Mr. Finch, now a Roseland family friend and a boarder at the bed and breakfast inn that Angie's sister, Ellie, ran out of the Victorian, sat in the front passenger seat. Angie propped her bike's kickstand and went to help Mr. Finch from the car.

"What a wonderful day." Finch grasped Angie's arm and leaned on his cane. He was still wearing the blue apron from the store he owned in town. "The candy store couldn't have been any busier."

"It's been a perfect opening day." Angie smiled as she helped Mr. Finch to the walkway that led to the gray house's front door.

The grand opening of the Finch and Roseland Confectioners was a huge hit with tourists and people from town swarming the store from the moment the doors opened. Mr. Finch had taken an hour break to come and see the house on Willow Street that had just come on the market. Angie's youngest sister, Courtney, co-owned the candy store with Finch and was taking care of business while he hurried off to look at the house.

Betty Hayes, dressed in a tan skirt and a black blazer, hustled over to where Angie and Finch stood on the walkway facing the gray Colonial. "I know it's fallen into disrepair, but I think it has great bones and I think you could nurse it back to health." Betty batted her eyelashes at Mr. Finch. "Shall we go in, Victor?" She reached for the older man's hand.

Angie still couldn't believe that these two people were a couple. She wasn't sure, but she estimated that Mr. Finch was in his seventies and that he must be ten years older than the ambitious Realtor who had caught his eye. The two had been dating for over a month and it was clear that they were smitten with each other.

"Here comes Miss Jenna." Finch waved at the tall brunette emerging from the group of trees at the back of the house.

Jenna jogged across the lawn to meet them. "Did you just get here? I had a customer in the shop and was afraid I'd miss seeing the house with you. I cut through the back yard to save time." Jenna ran a jewelry shop in one of the rooms at the rear of the Victorian.

"We all just arrived." Angie was a few inches shorter than her fraternal twin sister and had honey-colored hair in contrast to Jenna's long, brown locks. People always guessed that they were sisters, but never believed that the two were twins.

"The listing Realtor just put the house on the market. She had to leave town for a family emergency and she'll be gone for several months so a new Realtor and I are taking over some of her listings." Betty pressed the buttons on the lock box attached to the front doorknob. The box's lid slid back and Betty removed the door key. "We're the first ones to see the house." She waved her arm indicating the yard. "It's a good-sized lot, and as you know, it's walking distance to the center of town and a few blocks to the beach which makes it a very valuable property." Betty pushed the door open and stepped into the small foyer.

Mr. Finch followed and Angie and Jenna took up the rear. There was a staircase leading to the second floor directly in front of them.

"This is the living room on the left and the dining room to the right. There are three large bedrooms upstairs and two full baths."

Both the living and dining rooms had wood floors and there was a fireplace on the far wall, but the place was dusty and smelled of stale air from being closed up for so long. Garish floral wallpaper covered the walls.

A strange feeling of unease washed over Angie as she followed the others to the kitchen. The cabinetry was old pine board and the floor was covered with dingy linoleum. The windows were grimy and the light had a hard time filtering into the room.

"The kitchen needs work, but it's all cosmetic." Betty walked to a door on the side of the space and opened it to reveal a three-season sunroom right off the kitchen. "This is a bonus. Imagine sitting out here on a summer evening with a glass of wine or a cup of tea." She smiled sweetly at Finch.

"It's a beautiful room." Finch stood in the center of the space and pivoted, leaning on his cane, taking in the six sliding glass doors. He glanced into the back yard. "Very nice foliage and the trees along the property line provide good privacy." He winked at the girls. "You never know what kind of neighbors might be lurking back there behind those trees."

Jenna chuckled. "I'm sure the four sisters who live there are nothing but trouble."

Betty led the group into the kitchen and rattled on about how Finch could have the cabinets torn out and replaced, and the linoleum ripped up and wood floors put down.

Angie walked back into the living room and stood by the fireplace. Her sense of dread was growing and she couldn't reconcile her feelings of anxiety with being related to the deteriorated condition of the home. Something else besides the rundown, dated décor was responsible for the panicky pricks itching at her skin. Angie's heart pounded and her breathing was shallow and quick. She tried to tune in to what her senses were trying to tell her. Her ears buzzed, and even though she could hear Betty's voice, it sounded hollow and far away.

"Here's the first floor full bathroom on the left, and at the end of the hall there's a good-sized bedroom that you can use for the master so you won't need to be climbing stairs at night."

Angie turned away from the fireplace and looked to the hall just as Betty led Mr. Finch and Jenna towards the bedroom.

"Jenna." Angie's voice had a breathless, shrill edge to it that caused her sister to stop and stare at her.

Jenna's eyes narrowed. She whispered. "What's wrong with you?"

"I don't know. Something's not right." Angie's face had lost its color. She took three steps forward. "Something's bad in here."

Jenna moved quickly to her sister's side and touched her arm. "Should we get out?"

Betty and Mr. Finch were entering the first floor bedroom. "It's very dark in this room." Betty fumbled along the wall for a light switch.

A flash of searing light blazed in Angie's brain. She screamed, "Stop! Mr. Finch, don't go in there!" She rushed towards him.

Betty's eyes bugged out as Angie flew into the room and pushed the woman away from the wall. Angie whirled to Mr. Finch, clutched his arm, and pulled him into the living room. "Betty, get out of that room. Don't touch anything."

In the living room, three faces stared at Angie. She was panting and her shoulders were shaking.

"What on earth is wrong with you?" Betty's forehead was creased. She had a hand on her hip waiting for an explanation.

Jenna herded Finch and Betty out of the house. She looked at Angie. "Come on. Let's get some fresh air."

Outside, standing on the weedy lawn, Betty's face was bright red and her eyes flashed. "What was that all about?" Annoyance rang in her voice and she flapped her hand in the air for emphasis. Betty didn't wait for an answer. She pulled out her phone and whirled towards her car.

Angie sank onto the grass. Mr. Finch stepped closer and looked at the shaky young woman. Clutching his cane, he leaned down and whispered. "Is there danger, Miss Angie?"

Angie lifted her white face to the man. She nodded and turned to Jenna. "Call Police Chief Martin."

CHAPTER 2

Angie was on her feet by the time the chief's police car turned down Willow Street and pulled into the driveway. Betty was in her car speaking into her phone and gesturing animatedly, as she rearranged an appointment with a client. She'd complained loudly that valuable time was being taken out of her busy day due to someone's silly "feeling" that something wasn't right in the house. Although Mr. Finch assured Betty that intuition should always be respected, he knew Angie's "feeling" was more than a case of simple instinct.

Chief Martin crossed the lawn and made eye contact with Angie and Jenna. He was well aware that the Roseland sisters could sometimes sense things and he took their input seriously. "What's wrong with the house?"

Angie shrugged. "We were inside looking around. I got a funny feeling." She started to dismiss her sensation, but the chief interrupted her.

"I would never ignore a warning you've

experienced. I'm going to investigate the premises." Chief Martin glanced to the open front door. "Do you want to go inside with me and check it out? Show me where you were when you got the sensation of danger?"

Angie's eyes widened like saucers and she cringed at the thought of returning to the house.

Chief Martin picked up on her reaction. "Okay then. No one is to enter the house until it's been thoroughly inspected. I'll have two more officers come over and I'll call the town's building inspector." He went to his cruiser and spoke into his radio.

"I'm glad we have Chief Martin around." Jenna watched him making the arrangements to begin an inspection. "He takes us seriously."

"I feel a little silly." Angie ran her hand over the top of her head to smooth her hair. "It's probably nothing and I've caused all this hoopla."

Jenna gave her sister a serious expression. "Have your sensations ever been wrong?"

Angie pondered that for a few moments. "I guess not?" She frowned. "I hope it's wrong this time. It will just mean trouble. I thought we could just relax for a few months and not have some worry on our minds."

Jenna took a look at the house. "Well, maybe there's just a dead body in there."

A horrified look washed over Angie's face. "A dead body? That will lead to a huge investigation.

9

Who is it? How did they die? Was it foul play?
Blah blah."

Jenna sent a text to Courtney at the candy shop
and to Ellie at the B and B to inform them of the
latest crisis. "But a dead body won't involve us."

"Won't it?" Angie muttered as she stood up and
brushed pieces of grass from her butt. "Somehow I
doubt that."

Mr. Finch approached the girls. "Betty is going
to return me to the candy store. I don't want to be
away for very long on the shop's first day."

"I'm sorry I ruined your viewing of the house."
Angie held Mr. Finch's arm and walked him to the
car.

"Not to worry, Miss Angie. If you think I would
ever doubt you, you would be very wrong. Anyway,
things were becoming boring." Finch winked at
Angie. "We've had an hour or two without a
mystery to solve." His comment elicited a smile
from the young woman holding his arm. Taking his
seat in the vehicle, Finch said, "Be sure to call me or
Courtney if anything exciting turns up."

Angie shut the passenger side door. Finch spoke
through the open car window. "You and Jenna
can't have all the fun, you know." He waved to the
sisters as the car pulled away.

"Betty left without saying goodbye," Jenna
joked. "I don't think you're on her favorite person
list at the moment."

Angie rolled her eyes. "What makes you say

that?"

Chief Martin came up to the girls. "Why don't you two head home? I'll text you with any news. No use waiting around here."

"Okay." Angie nodded. "Let us know." She and Jenna headed for the tree line behind the Colonial house to cut through the trees to their backyard. Angie looked over her shoulder and called to the chief as she walked away. "Be careful in there."

Angie and Jenna opened the back door of the Victorian and entered the kitchen. Ellie stood at the counter cutting up strawberries, slices of honeydew melon, cantaloupe, and chunks of watermelon to make a fruit salad for her B and B guests. Her blonde hair was plaited in a long braid down her back. "What was the issue at the house?"

"They're investigating." Angie took a jug of iced tea from the refrigerator and filled a glass.

"It's not going to blow up or anything is it?" Ellie went on with her chopping.

Something skittered down Angie's back. Her eyes widened. She stared at Ellie. "Why did you say that?"

"I was just making conversation." When she saw the look on Angie's face, Ellie put the knife on the counter. "Oh, no." She glanced out the back window into the yard. "Are we in danger? Should we go down in the basement? Is it going to blow up?"

Tom pushed back the plastic sheet that was

draped between the kitchen and the small room he was renovating. He had knocked the wall down between the spaces to enlarge the kitchen area to provide more room to accommodate Angie's bake shop needs. "What's going on now?"

Euclid, their huge orange cat and Circe, the girls' black cat with a little white spot at her neck, walked into the kitchen with Tom. The felines jumped on the counter and then up to the top of the refrigerator where they perched listening to the conversation.

Jenna carried a cup of coffee to Tom and told him about the latest goings-on. She said to Ellie, "I think it's just a dead body in the house somewhere."

Ellie fiddled with the end of her braid. "*Just*? Just a dead body? How long has it been in there?"

Angie put her glass of iced tea on the counter. She took a deep breath. "We're only speculating. If there was a body, there would have been an odor. We didn't smell anything."

"Really?" Jenna scrunched up her nose. "It smelled bad in there."

"It was because the house had been shut up for so long. It was musty."

Tom leaned against the counter. He took a swallow of his coffee. "So the police and the inspector are checking it out?"

Angie was about to answer when her phone buzzed. "It's Chief Martin." She raised her eyes from the phone. "He wants us to come back."

Ellie shook her head. "I'm going to stay here. In case the guests need something."

The sisters knew that Ellie's reluctance to join them was only partially due to her concerns about her guests.

"Did Chief Martin say anything else? Give a hint about what they found?" Jenna headed for the backdoor.

Angie followed her sister. "Nothing else. He just said to come back to the house." She called over her shoulder. "We'll let you know what he says."

"I don't think I want to know," Ellie muttered. "Be careful, you two." She returned to cutting up the fresh fruit.

The girls hurried across the Victorian's backyard and headed for the trees. They ducked under branches and emerged onto the rear lawn of the Colonial house. Chief Martin stood in the driveway speaking with the inspector and when he spotted the girls, he walked towards them. His stride looked a little unsteady.

"So." He dabbed at his sweaty brow with a white handkerchief. The girls wanted him to hurry and tell them what he knew, but he was hesitating. "Angie, was there anything specific you were feeling when you were in the house?"

Angie's heart sank. They must not have found anything. That's why the chief was questioning her about what she'd felt. She swallowed. "Danger. That something in there was wrong, something was off."

"Specifically?" Chief Martin's eyes narrowed.

"Nothing specific, no." Her voice was soft. She felt foolish and guilty to have made such a commotion over something she wasn't even sure was real.

"Any place in the house that seemed particularly more ... uh, dangerous or worrisome?"

"You *did* find something, didn't you?" Jenna wondered why the chief seemed to be dancing around whatever discovery they'd made.

The chief didn't reply to her question.

"Wait." Jenna looked at her sister. "You told Betty and Mr. Finch to get out of that room, the first floor bedroom. That's when you got the most agitated, when we headed for the bedroom. You pulled Mr. Finch out of there."

Angie looked blank. She'd forgotten the details of the experience, but Jenna's comments drew some things from her memory. "Right," she said slowly. "It was that room." She looked towards the house. "The bedroom." A flood of anxiety rushed through her veins. "When we were in the house, there was a flash ... a bright, white light flashed in my head for second. I knew we had to get out of there."

Jenna and Angie repeated what they'd told the chief earlier. Angie had yelled for everyone to get out of the bedroom and Jenna, reacting to her sister's distress, shepherded all of them out of the house and into the yard.

The chief ran his hand across his forehead. "Well, it's a good thing you sensed something and you all got out without touching anything." The rate of his breathing seemed quick, faster than normal.

Jenna cocked her head. "What did you find?"

"The inspector, one of the officers, and myself ... we went inside. We looked things over, walked around." Sweat beaded on his upper lip. "The inspector found...."

"What?" Angie could barely stand to wait another second. "What was it?"

"The inspector found some wiring. Wiring that shouldn't be there." He took a deep breath. "The wiring was attached to the wall switch in the first floor bedroom."

"So, what was it?" Jenna's voice was husky.

"The wires traveled into the basement. They were attached to a bomb."

The girls' eyes nearly bugged out of their sockets.

"If someone flicked the wall switch...." Chief Martin mopped his forehead with the handkerchief.

Hoarse words escaped from Angie's throat. "What would have happened if the switch was flipped?"

Jenna's face was pale. "The house would have blown up?"

The chief nodded. "Along with anyone inside of it."

Angie's vision dimmed for a second and her ears buzzed from the realization of how close they'd come to being blown to bits. Betty Hayes was a moment from flicking the switch to light up the room. If she had turned the switch, it all would have ended by lighting up more than the bedroom.

Jenna grasped her sister's arm. "We came so close to getting...." Her words got stuck in her throat.

"Yeah. I feel the same way." Chief Martin took a deep breath. "All of you. The inspector, Officer Pratt, and I could have been blown to kingdom come. It's a sobering thought."

"It sure is." Jenna eyed the gray house and shuddered.

Angie tried to collect herself, but her hands trembled. "How on earth did a bomb get attached to the light switch?" The shock of what might have happened began to wane and a tidal wave of questions rose in her mind. "Who would do such a thing? Why would someone do that?" Cold drops of sweat ran down her back, but hot anger bubbled up inside her. She knew that the questions she was posing were unanswerable, for now anyway. She focused her thoughts. "Who owns this house? How long did they live here? How long has the place been empty? Where are the owners now?"

A little smile played over Chief Martin's lips. "Which one should I answer first?"

Jenna pushed her hair back. "Do you know the

answers to Angie's questions?"

"Some of them." The chief crooked a thumb into his waist band. "I suspect she'll have more to ask in a few seconds, so I'll start to tell you what I know. The house is owned by Chip and Elise Cook. They lived here in the summers for about twenty years. Now they're both in a retirement home. From what I understand, they haven't been able to use this house for a couple of years."

Angie asked. "It's been empty for two years?"

The chief nodded. "I believe so."

"That gave someone plenty of time to execute a plan of putting a bomb in the house." Angie kicked the dirt with the toe of her shoe.

"Any relatives?" Jenna asked.

"A son. He doesn't live around here. Name's Charlie. Charlie Cook."

Angie started another round of inquiry. "How old is Charlie? Where does he live? What does he do for a living? What took so long to put the house on the market?"

Chief Martin held up his hand to stop the onslaught of questions. "He lives in New Hampshire. Rye, I believe. I don't know the answers to your other questions. Yet."

Jenna asked, "Have you been in touch with the son?"

The chief nodded. "He's on his way down here." He looked at Angie. "Would you and your sisters like to sit in on my interview? Maybe you can get a sense of him."

"I don't think I'd be of any help." Jenna turned to her sister. "And it would be like dragging Ellie to the gallows to get her to agree to listen to the interrogation, but Courtney might be able to help, she might get some insight."

"Okay. Good suggestions." The chief looked at Angie. "What do you think?"

Angie did not want to get involved in the case. She wanted a nice quiet few weeks until Tom finished the renovations and she could open her bake shop again. She and her three sisters had been straight out the past couple of months with the girls moving to Sweet Cove, Angie closing her shop, Jenna and Ellie starting businesses out of the house, and Courtney and Mr. Finch opening the candy store in town.

That didn't take into account Angie inheriting the Victorian, the two murders in town, and the misdeeds of a long-dead relative they'd investigated. Angie longed for some peace and quiet, but it didn't look like that was going to be a reality any time soon. She knew she couldn't say no to Chief Martin, since she felt a duty to assist in any way possible. A reluctant sigh slipped from her lips. "I guess so. It couldn't hurt for me and Courtney to listen to what Charlie Cook has to say."

"There's one other thing. It seems the bomber wasn't content to wait until someone flicked the light." The chief mopped his brow again. "Not only was the bomb wired to the switch. It was set to blow up tonight. At midnight."

CHAPTER 3

Jenna and Angie opened the door to the candy store to see Mr. Finch placing a tray of sweets into one of the glass display cases.   His pleasant expression turned to concern when he saw the twin sisters enter his store.

"You found out what caused your worry?"   He stepped around the counter.

"We did."   Angie was almost relieved that the whole thing wasn't a goose-chase and that her feelings of danger had validity.   "Is Courtney in back?"

Jenna headed to the work room in back of the store to fetch her youngest sister.   "We may as well explain it to both of you at the same time."

Courtney came out wiping her hands on a cloth. "Mr. Finch told me what happened at the house. What have you discovered?"

Angie and Jenna went over the details that Chief Martin had shared with them about the bomb in the basement of the Willow Street home that was wired to go off when the first floor bedroom switch was flicked on.

"Shoosh." Courtney pulled over a stool and sat down. "That was a close call." She eyed her sisters and Finch. "What if ...?" The words stuck in her throat and her eyes went wide with the horror that could have been.

"Don't even say it." Angie's face had lost some of its color imagining how near they had come to losing their lives. "And, that's not all. The bomb was set to explode at midnight."

Jenna's shoulders drooped. "What kind of a nut would do such a thing?"

Mr. Finch touched the girls' arms and gently nudged them to the backroom. "Let's go sit in back. I'll make us all lattes. We can chat about this latest development." Mr. Finch had installed a latte machine in the candy making room so that he and Courtney and their employees could have tasty drinks while they worked. He bustled around taking out small white cups and working the buttons on his new machine. He delivered steaming beverages to each of the sisters and made one for himself. "Ah, much better." He sipped. "Now, let's discuss this case."

Angie told Courtney, "Chief Martin wants us both to be there when he talks to the son of the elderly couple who own the house. The son's name is Charlie Cook. He's on his way down here from New Hampshire. The Chief wants us to see if we can pick up on anything when we see the guy."

"That's a very good idea," Finch agreed.

Courtney paced about the room holding her coffee cup in her hand. "I think there's an equally important question as *who* did it. We should also be asking who the target was."

Jenna sat up. "We didn't even discuss that. We were so focused on the bomb and what could have happened."

"I asked a lot of questions, but that wasn't one of them." Angie blinked. "I should have thought about the intended victim and who it might be." She looked at Courtney. "Good thinking."

Courtney smiled and raised an eyebrow. "I don't watch crime shows for nothin', you know." She stopped at the built-in desk, sat down, and picked up a pen and piece of paper. "Let's write some things down. Just to keep it all straight." She moved the pen across the paper. "To start with, there's a bomb in the cellar rigged to go off when the bedroom light switch is turned on. Also, the bomb was set to ignite at midnight."

Jenna piped up. "The couple who owns the house is in a retirement home."

"What does that mean?" Courtney asked. "Are they in an assisted living place? A nursing home? Does that mean they're mentally incapacitated?"

"The chief didn't specify." Angie finished her latte and placed the empty cup on the counter. "That's something we should ask about. It might be helpful to talk to the couple, if it's possible."

"Do we know anything about the son, Charlie Cook?" Courtney tapped the pencil against her chin.

"No, we can ask about him when we go to the police station."

"I wonder how long the bomb has been in place." Mr. Finch's eyebrows furrowed. "That might help to narrow down who the intended target was. Perhaps Miss Betty Hayes can help by telling us when the house was last occupied. Maybe she can give us a list of people who have been in there since the house was put on the market."

"That could be telling. It could certainly widen the list of targets." Jenna went to the sink to rinse out her cup. "In fact, the target could be Betty herself."

Mr. Finch's mouth dropped open.

"It's a long shot." Angie tried to reassure him. "Betty isn't the listing agent."

Finch turned to Angie. "She is though. She and Brian Hudson, a Realtor new to Sweet Cove, are the listing agents. The original agent had a family emergency that called her out of town. Since she'll be away all summer and into the fall, she passed the listing to Betty and Brian to handle."

"When did this happen?" Jenna asked.

"Just a few days ago." Mr. Finch's face was pinched.

Angie asked, "But who would know Betty and

Brian had the listing if they only got it a few days ago?"

"Everyone would. It's on the website." Mr. Finch sat down hard. "It lists their names as the agents to contact. It's on both the website and on the house's listing information."

"Someone would have had to act fast to get a bomb in the house in a couple of days." Jenna shook her head. "How long would it take to install something like that?"

Courtney narrowed her eyes. "Probably not very long."

Angie walked over to the desk. "We need to tell Chief Martin about this. Make sure he warns Betty and Brian about the possibility that they could be the target."

Mr. Finch took his phone from the desk. "I will warn Miss Betty right now."

Angie sat in the chair next to Courtney. "Maybe you should write down possible targets of the bomb."

Courtney nodded and pointed to the paper she was writing on. "I already started. I put Betty's name right at the top."

The corners of Finch's eyes creased with worry as he stepped into the front room to make his call to Betty Hayes.

Jenna kept her voice low. "It's not out of the realm of possibility that someone might have it in for Betty." She glanced at the doorway to the front room to be sure Finch wasn't within earshot. "She can be very abrasive. And you know she would do anything to get a listing. I'm not saying she's unscrupulous, but she may push the boundaries."

Angie agreed. "She could easily have made an enemy. A client, maybe even a colleague. Some people are crazy and would do anything to get back at someone for a perceived slight or injustice."

Courtney thought of the two recent murder cases in town. "Isn't that the truth?"

"And we don't know Brian Hudson." Angie fiddled with her latte cup. "He or Betty could have an enemy."

"At least we're all safe and nothing happened to us when we were at that house." Jenna blew out a sigh of relief.

Courtney narrowed her eyes. "We need to keep our wits about us until this is solved. There is no way that we're going to end up being anyone's collateral damage."

Jenna's eyebrows shot up. "You don't think it's a nut, do you? Placing bombs here and there, just for kicks? Maybe the person doesn't care who his target is. Maybe he just wants to hurt people and scare everyone else."

"Yikes," Angie whispered. "That would be a different kind of case altogether."

"We need to tell Ellie what's going on," Courtney said. "Some new people have checked into the B and B in the past few days. Any one of them could be the bomber."

Angie didn't like the idea that some crazy person was living under the same roof with them. An idea popped into her head. "Could Mr. Finch be the target?"

"What?" Jenna asked incredulously. "Why?"

"He's living in the carriage house apartment. It's close to the property line. If the Willow Street house blew up, could it take out the carriage house, too?"

Courtney said, "What about the Victorian? Depending on the size of that bomb, would we have been at risk?"

"We should talk to Tom about all of this," Jenna suggested. "He might have some knowledge that could answer some of these questions."

"We need to talk to Chief Martin, too." Angie turned to see Mr. Finch returning from making his phone call. "How did Betty take the idea of being at risk?"

Finch's face was drawn. "She pooh-poohed the idea as being nonsense. Betty said she's been in business for forty years and has annoyed many people over that time, and nothing has ever happened to her." Finch shook his head. "Somehow her comments about how many people she has annoyed did not ease my mind."

Angie was about to say something comforting when her phone buzzed. She glanced at the screen and read the text, then looked up. "It's Chief

Martin.   Mr. Charlie Cook has arrived in Sweet Cove."

CHAPTER 4

Jenna stayed at the candy store to help Mr. Finch until the late afternoon employee came in to work so that Courtney could accompany Angie to the police station. Ellie said she would watch the jewelry shop until Jenna returned to the Victorian.

Angie and Courtney made their way into the lobby of the station. Chief Martin was off to the side speaking with an officer, but when he saw the girls arrive, he cut his conversation short and hurried over.

"I'm glad you could come by on such short notice. Mr. Cook is waiting in one of the conference rooms." He gestured for the girls to walk with him down the hallway. "I'll ask questions. I'd like you to listen and see if you pick up on anything or get any sort of feedback from Mr. Cook that might be floating on the air." The chief had a hard time verbalizing what he hoped the girls could sense, but they understood what he wanted them to do.

"Okay, we'll try and pick up on any currents

or feelings that Mr. Cook might give off." Angie made an effort to relax her muscles as they made their way to the conference room. She thought it best not to be tense or distracted in order to be open to whatever might show itself. She still had no idea how to control her "feelings" or how best to sense what people might give off and it left her feeling vulnerable.

The chief knocked on a closed door and a man's voice invited them in. Chief Martin held the door for the girls and Mr. Cook looked surprised when he saw the two women come into the room with the chief.

He stood up as Chief Martin made introductions. Cook looked fit and lean and Angie estimated that he must be in his mid-forties. The man had a good head of dark brown hair and wide, brown eyes.

The chief indicated that Angie and Courtney should take the two chairs on the same side of the table where he would sit.

When everyone was seated, Cook faced the girls. "Are you Police officers?"

Angie didn't know how to answer, so she hesitated trying to come up with a plausible explanation for their presence in the room.

Courtney jumped in. "We're criminal justice consultants to the Sweet Cove Police Department." She sat up straight and calmly folded her hands on the table in front of her. She gave off a professional manner and Angie thought that if this was the first time she'd met her sister, she would believe whatever Courtney said to her.

"So, Mr. Cook," the chief began. "I'm sorry to meet under these unusual circumstances."

Cook nodded.

Chief Martin went on. "If you could give us a bit of your background, please?"

Cook adjusted in his seat. "I'm Charlie Cook, forty-three years old. I was born and raised in a town right outside of Boston. I've worked as a teacher in the same high school in New Hampshire for over twenty years."

"Any siblings?"

"No. I'm an only child."

"Can you tell us about your parents?" The chief scribbled notes on a pad.

"My mother, Elise, has Alzheimer's and is a resident in a nursing facility in Wayland, Massachusetts. She's been there for about five years. My father, Chip, his real name is Charles, moved into the assisted living section of the facility. I understand that his health is okay. He has a cottage at the facility. Living there allows him to be close to my mother and receive any care he might need down the road."

"How long did your parents own the Sweet Cove house?"

Cook pondered. "I was in my senior year of high school when they made the purchase, so I'd say they owned it for about twenty-five years?"

"They spent summers here?" Chief Martin continued making notes from the conversation.

"Mother did. Father dropped in now and then. He didn't care for the beach. He didn't like tourists either. He bought the house because Mother wanted it."

"How about you? Did you make use of the place?"

Cook shook his head. "Really? I think I might have stayed there a handful of times, that's it."

"Are you and your parents close?"

Cook snorted. "No. We're not. I'm not sure when I saw them last to be honest." He rubbed his face and looked at Angie and Courtney. "My father told me about his move to assisted living by sending me a card in the mail announcing his change of address." He let out a sigh. "I'm sure that sounds terrible to you."

Since there wasn't any good way to respond to that statement, the girls just gave tiny, sympathetic smiles as if they didn't really have an opinion one way or the other.

"Did your parents have any enemies, any people who might hold ill will towards them?" Chief Martin made eye contact with Mr. Cook.

"I couldn't say. I doubt Mother had anyone who wished her ill. She had a few close friends. She never worked outside the home. She liked needlework, sewing, cooking, gardening, things like that. She was a quiet, solitary person and seemed

31

happy with the way things were." He folded his arms over his chest. "Father is a different story. I wouldn't be surprised if someone wanted to do him in." He chuckled, but there was no smile on his face. "That very thought crossed my mind once or twice when I was a young man."

Chief Martin raised his eyebrows.

"Not to worry, Chief. It was only a passing fancy, nothing I would ever have acted on. My father and I didn't get along. Father was a successful businessman. He wanted me to follow in his footsteps. I didn't, and that did not go over well with him." Cook sighed. "My father and I were complete opposites. I really didn't know the man, not when I was young and certainly not now."

"Did you know your parents had put the house up for sale?"

"No. I don't care either. My father cut me out of his will a long time ago. He made that bit of information very clear to me. What they do with their property is no concern of mine."

Angie felt a slight twinge at Cook's last statement, but she couldn't tell if she thought it was a lie that he didn't care or it was something else.

"Why did you call me about the problem with the house?" Cook asked.

"I called your father's phone a couple of times. He didn't answer. Your name is listed as the second contact on the listing contract."

Cook laughed. "Why in the world would that be?

You'd better call and speak to my father. It's his house. Since you called me, I assumed something must have happened to my father, so I came down to help you out."

"I will call him right after our meeting." The chief looked at his notes and then looked up. "Would you mind staying in town overnight, maybe a couple of nights? Just for some follow-up. The house is being inspected tomorrow morning by an expert from Boston, just to be sure there isn't anything else of concern set up in the house."

Cook frowned. "I guess I could. I assume the house is off limits to me?"

Chief Martin nodded. "The department would be happy to cover the cost for any nights you need to be here in town." He flicked his eyes to Angie and Courtney. "There's a very nice bed and breakfast inn close by. When we're done here, I'll check with the proprietor to see if there is a room available."

Angie's eyes widened. She didn't expect the chief to put Cook up at the Victorian.

Cook made eye contact with each sister. "Don't you have any questions for me?"

Courtney tilted her head and gave Cook a piercing look. "We listen."

Angie wanted to smile, but held back. Hearing her sister's tone of authority made her realize that anyone who heard Courtney speak would accept what she told them as fact.

After the meeting, Angie called Ellie to inquire if the B and B could accommodate another guest and Chief Martin gave Charlie Cook directions to several town restaurants.

Angie clicked off from her sister and approached the chief. "Ellie says she has a room for Mr. Cook."

"He just left. I'll send him over to the B and B when he comes back after he gets something to eat." The chief took Angie's arm and moved her down the hall so no one could hear their conversation. His voice was barely above a whisper. "Did you sense anything?"

"I'm not sure. I didn't get any strong thrumming to indicate danger, but I felt a twinge of something when Cook talked about his mother and when he denied caring about being cut out of the will. That could just be any normal person's reaction to what he said though ... not necessarily anything, you know...." she glanced over her shoulder, "paranormal." She looked around. "Where's Courtney?"

Right on cue, her sister came walking towards them from the restroom. "Hey Sis, what's cookin'? Get it? *Cook*"-in. As in, Mr. Cook."

Angie and Chief Martin shook their heads at Courtney's lame joke.

Courtney ignored them. "What did we think of him?"

Angie told her of the mild twinges she got from Cook.

"Well, I think he's hiding something." Courtney crossed her arms over her chest.

"Is this just your guilty until proven innocent thing?" Angie turned towards the chief and smiled. "Courtney has a backwards interpretation of our justice system."

Courtney cocked her head. "Say what you will. I think he's hiding something."

"Is this a 'feeling'?" Angie moved her fingers in the air miming quotation marks. "Or is it a normal thing that anyone would sense?"

"I think it's both."

"By the way," Angie told her sister. "I was very impressed by the way you presented yourself in the meeting."

Courtney winked. "I'm a good actress, aren't I?" She threw her shoulders back and put her nose in the air. "I am a criminal justice consultant." She chuckled. "Whatever that is."

"Mr. Cook didn't question what you said, so good work pretending you are something you're not." Angie gave her sister a playful bop.

"I hope you don't mind that I suggested the B and B," Chief Martin said. "I thought it best to keep Mr. Cook under surveillance, if you know what I mean."

"We'll do our best to get to the bottom of Mr. Cook and his motives." Courtney smiled. "I want to see what the cats think of him."

Chief Martin cleared his throat. "Um, yes …

good." The chief knew the cats sensed things, but he was still uncomfortable about it and never knew how to address their skills. But neither did anyone else. "Well, thanks for coming down and sitting in on the discussion. We'll talk tomorrow. Keep your eyes on Cook once he shows up at the B and B."

Courtney raised an eyebrow and gave a sly smile. "Mr. Cook has probably never in his life been as scrutinized as he is going to be this evening. Leave it to us."

As they were heading down the steps of the police station, Courtney turned to Angie. "I still think Chief Martin should deputize us. I'd really like a silver badge."

Angie shook her head and put her arm over her sister's shoulders. "I think you'll have a long wait."

CHAPTER 5

Courtney and Angie sat at the kitchen table reporting to Ellie, Jenna, Mr. Finch and Tom what went on at the police station. They discussed the strangeness of the incident at the Willow Street house, who might have done it, and who might be the target. They also talked about the possibility that the bomb was placed randomly. Euclid and Circe sat side-by-side on top of the refrigerator listening to the humans converse.

Most of the kitchen renovations had been completed. Tom finished one side of the room so that the girls could prepare meals there instead of going back and forth to one of the carriage house kitchens. Although he still had finish work to do on that side, and more to complete on the far side, everyone, especially Ellie, was happy to have a useable space again.

"So when Cook shows up here, we need to keep our eyes on him. Engage him in conversation. We need to try and remember what he says, no matter how trivial it may seem. That way, we can dissect it later." Courtney looked at Angie. "I'm hungry. What are we making for dinner?"

Angie went to the refrigerator and took out ground beef, veggies, and sauces. She reached for some spices from the cabinet. "Let's do burgers and veggie burgers. It will be fast and simple, so then we'll be ready when Mr. Cook shows up."

"I'll chop the veggies." Courtney pulled out a strainer and washed the vegetables in the sink.

"How about some rice and a green salad to go with the burgers?" Jenna offered to prepare them.

"May I be of assistance?" Mr. Finch asked. His eyelids looked droopy. The candy store opening day had exhausted him and the girls were sure that his worry over Betty Hayes being a possible target of the bomb was contributing to his fatigue.

Courtney knew how much Mr. Finch liked to help, so she brought a small cutting board over to where he was sitting. She carried some mushrooms and peppers to the kitchen table. "Here, you can chop these while you sit."

"You know, Miss Courtney, I'm never one to sit down on the job." Finch gave her a little smile as he picked up the knife she'd brought to him. "After dinner, I'll walk up to the candy store and check on the employees."

"Why don't I do that?" Courtney suggested. "I'll go check on the store right after we eat." She knew her candy partner was worn out from the day and she thought it best if Mr. Finch relaxed for the

38

evening. "Anyway, since you're the only man around here, except for Euclid and he can't talk, maybe it would be best if you stayed for a while after dinner and tried to engage Mr. Cook in conversation."

Euclid meowed.

Tom stood on the other side of the kitchen making adjustments to the new cabinet doors. "*I'm a man, by the way.*"

Courtney chuckled. "I didn't think you'd still be here after dinner."

"Will you stay for a while?" Jenna asked Tom. "Maybe you and Mr. Finch could chat with Mr. Cook and get some information out of him."

Tom winked at Jenna. "Well, since it's you asking me to stay, I'd be glad to."

Jenna knew that Tom had worked highway and road construction before he started his renovation business. "What do you think about the house bomb? How much damage would it have caused?"

"It all depends on the size of the thing." Tom used a screwdriver to tighten a screw on the cabinet casing. "Of course, it obviously was built in order to destroy the house, so it must have had some oomph, and if there was an oil tank in the basement, well, that would add to the explosive power and start a huge fire. It could have been pretty bad. Maybe take out the house next to it, set the trees on fire." Tom paused and shook his head. "There easily could have been extensive damage to

J.A Whiting

the neighborhood area and loss of life." He made eye contact with Angie. "I didn't know, ah, how useful your ... 'gifts' could be. Thankfully, your intuition saved the day."

Jenna thought about the events of the past months. "The family 'skills' have certainly come in handy recently."

Courtney whirled around to Angie. "I know. Make a truth muffin, or a cake, or something. For Mr. Cook."

Angie stood at the stove. She gave her sister the evil eye. "No," she said firmly.

"What's this about?" Finch asked the question without looking up from his chopping task.

"It's nothing," Angie muttered.

Mr. Finch had been kept in the dark about Angie putting a "truth spell" on a muffin when he first arrived in Sweet Cove in order to get him to be more forthcoming about his relationship with his brother. It backfired terribly causing Finch to fall in love with Angie. Thankfully, he didn't recall any part of the misadventure.

Tom put down his screwdriver and walked over to the table. "It definitely sounds like something. In fact, it sounds like a very interesting story."

Finch raised his head and looked at each girl. The sisters had frozen in place with blank expressions on their faces.

"Perhaps I'd enjoy hearing the story about the truth muffin." Finch placed his knife next to the

40

chopped vegetables.

Angie sighed, and decided to tell Mr. Finch what they'd done to him. She hadn't liked keeping it a secret. Each sister took a turn relaying the events of the "truth muffin."

Tom and Finch roared with laughter at the tale and Finch had to dab at his eyes with a napkin from time to time from so much chortling.

Angie apologized profusely.

"I forgive you, Miss Angie." Finch spoke between chuckles.

"I won't ever do anything like that again." Angie's face was serious.

"Well," Courtney said to Finch with an impish grin. "At least she won't do it to *you* again."

Angie shook her head. "No. I don't know how to control it, so I won't be venturing into that territory again."

Courtney waved a hand in the air. "You just need to practice."

The phone in Angie's pocket buzzed. She checked the message. "It's Chief Martin. Mr. Cook is on his way over here to check in to the B and B."

Courtney looked at the little group in the kitchen and dramatically mimicked a drum roll. "Duh dun dun."

Everyone carried the dinner items to the dining table so that they could invite Mr. Cook to join them when he arrived. They took their seats and passed around the food.

J.A Whiting

"What's taking him so long?" Ellie asked. "I'm getting indigestion just waiting for him to ring the bell." As if on cue, the front door bell sounded.

"I'll get it." Courtney darted for the door, but collected herself before opening it. "Hello."

Cook's eyes widened with surprise, recognizing Courtney from the police station. "You're staying here?"

"I live here." Courtney stepped back so the man could enter.

Cook carried a small bag with the name of a town clothing store printed on the side. When he saw the group gathered around the table, eating, he said, "Oh, I've interrupted your meal."

Ellie stood, her long blonde hair tumbling down her back. She approached Mr. Cook and introduced herself. "I was expecting you. It's Mr. Cook, right? Chief Martin called and made arrangements." She smiled and gestured to the table. "Please join us."

"Oh, no." Cook shook his head. "I've eaten already."

Ellie said, "Have some dessert, then. Would you like some coffee or tea?"

"Thanks, but I'll pass."

Ellie wanted to throttle Cook. If he went up to his room and stayed there, they wouldn't have any chance to speak to him. She got an idea. "Your room isn't quite ready yet. Please, sit. We're having renovations done and my office has been

42

affected, so if you don't mind, I'll get you the guest registration card and you can fill it out at the table."

Cook nodded. "I didn't know I'd be staying overnight so I went to the store for some things. Can I leave it here?" He placed his bag in the corner of the foyer and reluctantly moved to the dining table.

Tom stood up and pulled out the chair next to him. He made introductions around the table and Cook sat down.

"How about some wine or beer?" Courtney stood to go to the kitchen.

Cook ran his hand through his short hair. "A beer sounds good."

Angie hoped Cook might have more than one beer with the idea that drinking might loosen his tongue. She wanted to start some discussion, so she told the group, "Mr. Cook is a teacher. He's from New Hampshire."

Mr. Finch smiled. "I worked as a teacher for several years. I taught mathematics."

Euclid sat at attention on top of the China cabinet. He gave Finch a look, but remained silent.

In fact, Mr. Finch had never been a teacher at all. When he'd first arrived in Sweet Cove, he told the girls that teaching had been his occupation before he retired, while in reality, he'd been something of a fortune-teller. He thought it best to keep that tidbit of information to himself until he got to know the family.

Cook nodded, but didn't say anything.

Finch prodded him. "What do you teach?"

"I work at a vocational school." Cook lifted his glass of beer to his mouth and took a swallow. "I prepare students to become electricians."

Euclid let out a low hiss.

Cook shifted his gaze to the top of the cabinet to see where the noise came from. "Oh. Cats," he said dismissively.

Angie stared at the man. *An electrician? That kind of knowledge would make it pretty easy to wire a bomb to a light switch.* "Have you worked as an electrician?"

"I'm licensed and keep up with the latest. I focus now on the teaching during the school year, but in the summer, I do electrical projects and consulting."

Angie glanced up at the felines. They sat straight and alert, staring intently at Cook.

Tom engaged the man in conversation and Jenna brought out a fruit pie that Angie made the day before. She sliced it and passed pieces around to everyone. Cook gratefully accepted. After a few bites, he said, "Excellent pie."

Angie thanked him and Cook looked at her. "You bake, too?"

Jenna didn't know that Angie and Courtney told Cook they were criminal justice consultants when they'd met him at the police station. She said, "Angie runs a bake shop. It's closed at the moment until the renovations are finished."

Cook tilted his head, confused. "I thought you were a criminal justice...."

Mr. Finch piped up to cover for Angie. "These women have many talents. They run multiple businesses and have several different degrees in a variety of fields. They are truly Renaissance women."

"Huh," was all Cook said to that. He took a swallow of his beer. He eyed the pie in the center of the table. Courtney cut and served him another piece.

Finch said, "We were sorry to hear about the trouble at your house."

Cook shook his head. "It's not my house."

"Still," Finch went on, "a family member's house. It's quite alarming."

"I think it's probably more alarming to all of you than it is to me since you live right behind the house." He chuckled. "Maybe you were the intended victims."

Euclid narrowed his eyes and let out a deep growl.

Ellie walked into the dining room with the registration card and a pen. "What?" Her tone was high-pitched and her eyes were wide. She stopped in her tracks. "Why would *we* be the target of the bomb?"

Cook shrugged. "Who knows? Whoever put it in the house couldn't be sure who would flick that switch.   Maybe the explosives were powerful enough to reach over here. Could be the intended victim, or victims, were nearby and not the unfortunate person who just happened to turn on the light in the bedroom."

Ellie exhaled loudly. "That seems a preposterous suggestion. The bomb couldn't reach all the way over here." She placed the guest information card next to Cook. "Would you mind filling this in?"

Cook started to register his information on the card.

Ellie sat down next to Cook. She would not give in to the suggestion that the bomb was intended for the Victorian. "Who on earth would want to put a bomb in your parents' house?"

"The police asked me the same question." Cook continued writing on the card without looking up.

Ellie pressed. "And did you have an answer for them?"

"What?" Cook looked up. "Oh, no, I didn't. Here you go." He handed the form to Ellie.

Tom commented. "You don't seem surprised by the bomb in the house."

"Who's surprised by anything these days? It's a nutty world." Cook tipped his glass of beer and swallowed the last bit. "I guess I'll head to my room."

Ellie handed him his key. "I'll show you where the room is."

Mr. Finch looked at the man. "Do you play
46

cards?"

Cook looked surprised. "Yeah, I do."

"Would you care to play after you've freshened up?"

"Well, sure. I guess I would." He checked his watch. "Say in an hour?"

"Very good. I'll meet you here at the table." Finch gave a slight nod.

Courtney leaned forward once Ellie and Cook were out of earshot. "How clever of you. How did you know he played cards?"

"I didn't. Unless, I picked up on it subconsciously. At any rate, I took a gamble since we didn't want him retiring to his room so soon."

Euclid trilled his approval. Circe climbed down off the China cabinet and jumped into Finch's lap for some patting.

Courtney observed the felines. "The cats don't seem to be thrilled with Mr. Cook, but their reaction isn't violently against him."

"I noticed that too," Angie said. "Maybe they're reserving judgment."

Jenna stood and started to clear the plates. "He didn't have much to reveal did he?"

"Maybe he doesn't really know anything." Angie stood up to help.

"Could that bomb have reached this far?" Ellie's face looked pale.

Tom said, "Well, it could, if..."

"Tom, it's best not to say anything on the

subject. It will just upset people." Jenna tilted her head towards Ellie so Tom would know what she meant.

"I was going to say that it would have to be a very big bomb, so it's highly unlikely that it would damage the Victorian." He patted Ellie's arm. "No need to worry."

Courtney grinned. "Remember who you're talking to. Ellie is the champion worrier of Massachusetts. Maybe even in the whole United States."

Ellie frowned at her sister. "I want us all to be safe."

"We are all safe," Tom said reassuringly. "The bomb has been dismantled."

After the dinner clean-up was completed, Jenna and Tom took coffee out to the front porch and sat in the rockers. Mr. Finch went into the living room with the cats to relax before the card game with Cook, and Ellie took her laptop into the family room to do some B and B paperwork.

Courtney shut the dishwasher door after filling it with the dinner dishes. "Want to walk up to the candy store with me? I'm going to go check on the employees and make sure everything is okay. I'm going to stay until closing. I don't like that we've been away from the store for a couple of hours. Our employees are experienced, so I know everything's okay, but I want to be sure."

Angie rinsed her tea cup in the sink and added it

to the dishwasher load. She pressed the button to start the cleaning cycle. "I'll go with you, but I want to be back in time for Mr. Finch and Cook's card game." She gave Courtney a look. "The last time I walked you to the candy store, we found dead Finch."

Mr. Finch's brother had run the candy store until last month when he was murdered by a Sweet Cove resident. Angie and Courtney found him in the rear of the store lying on his back with a knife sticking out of his gut. Dead Finch was a nasty, mean man who brought plenty of misery to the people around him, and the way he lived his life resulted in no one mourning his passing. The store was now owned by the "good" Mr. Finch and Courtney.

Courtney shook her head trying to dislodge the image of finding Finch murdered in the candy store. "Hopefully, everyone working at the store tonight is well, upright, and alive. Let's go."

CHAPTER 6

Courtney grabbed her wallet and she and Angie left the Victorian and headed up Beach Street to the center of town. The stars twinkled overhead and light from store windows streamed in pools on the sidewalks as couples strolled along hand in hand and families chatted to each other while eating ice cream cones or sipping drinks from take-out cups.

Courtney smiled. "I love tourist season."

Angie watched the people window-shopping, and coming and going from the stores and restaurants. She loved everything about Sweet Cove in the summer ... the weather, the hustle and bustle of all the people out and about, and the long, warm days. She let out a contented sigh.

As they approached the candy shop, Courtney said, "Look at all the people in the store. I thought things might slow down since we had so many customers during the day."

The girls put on aprons and joined the three employees waiting on patrons and ringing up sales. Angie thought the candy store was similar to her bake shop as customers eagerly picked out treats and their happy moods filled the air. It seemed that having sweets around usually put people in cheerful spirits.

After an hour passed, Courtney came into the customer area carrying a platter of new chocolates and placed them onto a shelf inside one of the glass display cases. She tried to stifle a yawn. "I never in a million years expected today to go so well." Just a few people remained in the store choosing some candy from the case on the far side of the room.

"It's been great." Angie ran a cloth over the top of the candy display. "I'm really happy for you and Mr. Finch."

The door opened and in walked Rufus Fudge, a young man from England who was interning for the summer with Attorney Jack Ford. He was tall and had brown hair and brown eyes, which had nearly fallen out of his head earlier in the day when he was at the store and met Courtney. Angie was not surprised to see him and was even less surprised at her sister's reaction when she saw Fudge. The two of them beamed at each other.

"How was your opening day?" Rufus asked.

"It was perfect. It couldn't have been better." Courtney thought that Rufus' arrival was the icing on a wonderful day.

"When I was here earlier, I noticed the shop's closing times near the front door."

Angie could see that Courtney's cheeks were

tinged with a slight bit of color and she bit her lip to keep from chuckling about how she would tease her later.

Rufus continued, "If you're not too tired from the busy day, I wondered if you'd fancy having a cup of tea somewhere with me?"

Courtney smiled and flashed her perfect row of white teeth. "I'd love a cup of tea."

Angie was pretty sure that the cup of tea wasn't what was attracting her sister to Rufus's proposition. She checked the time and thought she'd better get home to watch the card game between Mr. Finch and Charlie Cook. "I'm going to head home now."

"Oh." Courtney's eyes widened. "I should go with you. In case, you know, something seems off during the card game."

Rufus looked broken-hearted that Courtney might change her mind.

Angie took off her apron. "It's okay. You've been working hard. Go out for a drink and relax for a while. Mr. Finch will be there and the cats, too, if anything floats on the air." She tried to be as cryptic as possible so as not to alarm the young Englishman.

Rufus flicked his eyes between Courtney and Angie with a look of befuddlement, wondering what in the world the girls were saying to each other.

"Nice to see you again." Angie nodded to Rufus and left the store. She hurried home weaving around the people walking through town. When she opened the Victorian's front door, she expected to see Finch and Cook at the dining table engaged in a card game, but the room was empty. She checked the living room and then headed to the kitchen.

Finch and Ellie sat at the kitchen table with cups of tea and pieces of pie.

"What happened to the game?" Angie blinked.

"Hello to you, too." Ellie put a piece of the fruit pie into her mouth.

"I was stood up." Mr. Finch frowned. "Not really. Mr. Cook decided to decline the invitation in favor of heading to bed early."

"Oh." Angie sat down with them. Disappointment showed on her face. "You couldn't convince him to play one round?"

"I suppose we could have tied him to the chair." Ellie licked her fork.

Finch smiled at Ellie's comment. "The man was tired. There wasn't anything we could do."

Angie sighed. "Now, what?"

"Now I'm going up to my room to read for a little while." Ellie gathered the cups and plates from the table.

"I believe that I will retire as well. I am worn out from the day." Finch breathed a sigh. "It's a good feeling though."

"I'll walk you to the carriage house." Angie stood

up. "Clouds have rolled in. It's a dark night."

The cats jumped off the fridge so they could join Angie and Finch on the short stroll to his apartment in the carriage house. Finch grasped his cane, wished Ellie a good night, and followed Angie and the felines out the back door.

Angie took the older man's arm in case he stumbled on the darkened walkway. The lights were on at the back of the Victorian and near the entrance to the carriage house, but it was a dark night with some cloud cover hiding the moon.

"Any thoughts on what happened at the Willow Street house today?" Angie wanted Finch's opinion about the bomb.

"It was an appalling discovery. The behavior of some people is beyond my ability to comprehend." Finch leaned heavily on his cane.

"Any sensations of any kind?" Angie asked.

"None. I don't know why I didn't pick up on anything when Miss Betty was showing us around inside of the house. I should have been aware of the danger."

"You were focused on deciding if the place would be your home. You were distracted. It's understandable." Angie opened the door to the small entryway with the staircase that led up to the two apartments. "I don't always feel things either. Most of the time, I don't sense anything at all."

"Well." Finch straightened up and smiled. "Overall, it was an excellent day. The candy store was a success and we didn't get blown up by a bomb."

Angie grinned. "That's my definition of a very good day."

"Good night, Miss Angie." Finch started up the stairs to his apartment.

"Good night, Mr. Finch." Angie locked and shut the carriage house door. She turned to follow the walkway back to the Victorian when she noticed the cats weren't around. She called to them, trying to make out their shapes in the darkness. She edged over to the patio to see if the cats were on the lawn furniture.

"Circe? Euclid?" Angie glanced to the back entryway of the Victorian wondering if the animals had returned to the house. She couldn't see either one on the steps or anywhere in the dark yard. A rustling to her right made Angie turn her head towards the noise. She took several steps closer to the tree line at the rear of her property. A soft mew came from the bushes that were growing in clumps next to the trees.

"Euclid?" She wasn't sure why, but she whispered his name. She moved closer and spotted the orange cat under a bush. He was well-hidden except for his enormous raccoon-like tail sticking out from the foliage. She smiled. "You need to do a better job of hiding yourself."

Something caught Angie's eye on the other side of the thicket. She froze in place. Through the trees, she could see a light flickering near the back of the Colonial house they'd visited earlier in the day. Angie hunched over trying to get a better view through the thick leaves and bushes. Her heart pounded. She looked down and noticed Circe sitting next to Euclid. The black cat was staring at the light. Euclid glanced at Angie, and she put her index finger to her mouth to indicate the need for quiet. She slowly moved her feet further into the group of trees, gently pushing aside branches and being careful where she stepped so as not to alert whoever was moving around the outside of the house with a flashlight.

Angie wondered if the person in the Willow Street yard was a police patrolman inspecting the property to be sure no new funny business was going on inside or outside the home. The figure didn't appear to be wearing a uniform, but from her distance she couldn't be sure.

A bead of cold sweat ran down Angie's spine. What if this was the bomber returned to hide another explosive device? What if he's plotting to get inside and place another bomb at the house? Or maybe he has another idea for trouble.

Angie moved her trembling hand to her back pocket for her phone, thinking it would be best to alert Chief Martin to the backyard intruder with a text message. Her pocket was empty. She'd left the phone on the kitchen table.

As Angie pondered whether she should stay and

observe the person or hurry inside the Victorian to retrieve her phone, the flashlight beam shining on the grass started to head her way. Her breath caught in her throat. *Why is he coming this way?*

She looked over her shoulder to gauge the distance to the carriage house in case she had to make a run for it. The intruder would certainly see her if she moved, so deciding the safest thing to do would be to freeze in place, Angie took a slow, deep breath trying to calm her shaking body. She hoped her trembling limbs wouldn't give her away. She slid closer to the ground into the dark shadows and crouched down.

The man headed into the thicket of trees several yards to the right of the frightened young woman. *Please don't see me.* Her mind raced. *Why is he coming into our yard? Is he coming to check out the carriage house or maybe the Victorian? Is he planning to hide a bomb on our property?*

Angie's heart thundered. Her vision sparkled and her head buzzed. She hoped she wasn't about to pass out. She put her hand on the trunk of a tree and the rough bark against her skin seemed to steady her. She held her breath as the man walked parallel to her position and stepped out of the trees into the Victorian's back yard. He flicked off the flashlight.

She almost gasped when she saw his face in the glow from the light at the edge of the carriage house. *Charlie Cook!* She watched the man walk to the wraparound porch and head to the Victorian's front door.

What's he up to?

CHAPTER 7

Angie pushed past the tree branches and raced to the back steps of the house with the two cats running at her side. She burst into the kitchen, breathing hard.

Jenna whirled around. She was holding a bowl of ice cream in her hand. "What's wrong now?"

Angie tried to catch her breath. The cats jumped onto the kitchen table.

"I was in the back yard." Her chest heaved from a mix of fear and anger. "I saw Charlie Cook skulking around the Colonial house with a flashlight."

The girls heard footsteps in the foyer.

Angie whispered, "That's him. He came in the front door. He was sneaking around outside."

"I thought he went up to his room." Jenna put her bowl on the table and didn't notice as the cats moved over to it and took turns licking the ice cream.

"Maybe he did go to his room, but then he snuck out." Angie moved with purpose towards the hallway, but Jenna grabbed her sister's arm.

"Don't confront him now." Worry wrinkled Jenna's brow. "What if he loses his temper? What if he has a weapon?"

Angie blew some air out of her lungs, exasperated. She ran her hand over the top of her head. "You're right. I shouldn't approach him when I'm angry. I'll mention it to him in the morning when he comes down for breakfast. We'll all be here then. The other guests will be awake. There will be too many people around for him to do anything stupid."

Jenna nodded her approval. "We can watch his reaction when you tell him you saw him. See if he gets agitated or nervous. He'll make up some excuse and we'll try to figure out if he's hiding his real intention."

"Okay. That's the best way to go about this." Angie scowled. "What was he up to out there? It makes me nervous."

Jenna picked some leaves and little twigs out of Angie's hair. "Well, I figure we're safe for now. If he is the bomber, he isn't going to set anything off when he's here in the house."

Angie narrowed her eyes. "I guess that's *slightly* comforting." She glanced at the kitchen table. "The cats are eating your ice cream."

Jenna flew to the table and shooed them away. She lifted the bowl and looked at the contents. She turned, and with an innocent little grin, held the bowl out to her sister. "Want some?"

***

After both girls had a night of tossing and turning and thinking about Charlie Cook sneaking around the Willow Street house, Jenna and Angie stumbled sleepy-eyed into the kitchen to find Ellie buzzing around preparing for the guests' breakfasts. Blueberry pancakes cooked on one griddle and bacon sizzled on a second one.

"Yum." Jenna closed her eyes and inhaled the cooking smells. "Is there enough for me?"

Ellie used a spatula to lift three pancakes onto a plate. "There's always enough for my sisters." She handed the plate to Jenna. "You want some, Angie?"

Angie was making herself a cup of tea. "Thanks, but I think I'll just have cereal." She didn't want to upset Ellie, but she knew she had to tell her about what she saw last night. "After I walked Mr. Finch to the carriage house last night, I saw something."

Ellie turned away from the griddle holding the spatula in her hand. Worry formed little crinkles between her eyebrows. She waited to hear the rest.

Angie explained the details of what she saw.

Ellie turned and flipped some pancakes. "I think it's smart to act nonchalant when you talk to Cook. Tell him you noticed him coming back from the direction of the adjoining property last evening, and then we'll gauge his reply." She used tongs to place the bacon strips on some paper towels to drain off the grease. "It could be that Cook only wanted to walk around his parents' house and take a look at it. It's probably completely innocent."

"Cook is meeting with Chief Martin over at the house this morning." Jenna sipped her coffee. "Why didn't he just wait until then to look around? And Cook claims that he doesn't even care about that house, so why go off late at night to hoof around the place in the dark?"

Angie spooned cereal into her mouth. "We'll get to the bottom of it." She discussed with Ellie what she should bake for the guests and then set about mixing and spooning batter into muffin tins. "We should talk to Betty Hayes today just to cover all the bases. Ask her who she might have made into an enemy."

"If you help me with the jewelry tonight, I'll go with you to see Betty." Jenna poured a bit more maple syrup on her pancakes.

"Did anyone hear Courtney come in last night?" Angie placed a muffin tin on the middle rack of the oven.

"I heard her." Ellie stacked pancakes in a warming tray. "I was up late reading in my room. I thought she was with you."

Angie told her sisters about Rufus Fudge showing up at the candy store.

Ellie grinned. "She's in for some teasing."

Jenna nodded. "Too bad we have to wait until she gets home from work."

"It will give us time to think of some good lines to use on her." Angie carried a fruit bowl into the dining room.

The B and B guests gathered around the table and made pleasant chit chat with one another sharing information about their lives and travels. The guests included a retired couple, two middle-aged sisters, a woman in her fifties on her way to visit her daughter in Maine, and a newly-married couple taking a driving tour of New England. The guests spoke with the Roseland sisters about what to see in the area and places to have lunch and dinner.

When most of the guests were finishing their coffee and tea, Angie sidled up to Ellie. "Where's Mr. Cook? He hasn't come down for breakfast."

"I was wondering the same thing. Breakfast is almost over. I'll go up and knock on his door and see if he wants us to keep some breakfast items warm for him." She headed for the wide, carved wooden staircase. In a few minutes she was back, a scowl on her face. "There's no answer. Looks like our man has flown the coop. He didn't leave his key, so he'll be back."

Angie groaned. "I'll have to bring up his late night visit to his parents' house later today." She started to remove some empty platters from the buffet table that was placed on one side of the dining room. Something a few of the guests were talking about caught her attention and she pretended to be fiddling with things so she could listen.

Mrs. Roberts said, "Did you hear what happened yesterday on the street that runs behind this one?"

The guests revealed that they were in the dark about the events of the prior day.

Mrs. Roberts leaned into the table, eager to share the gossip. "There's a house for sale on that street. It's empty at present." She paused for effect. "The police found a bomb in the basement wired to go off when someone turned on a light switch."

The other guests let out gasps.

"And did you know there have been two recent murders in Sweet Cove?" Mrs. Roberts clearly loved being the bearer of bad news.

"I *did* know that." The newly-married young man spoke up. "I love murder mysteries. That's one of the reasons we came to visit this town."

Angie cringed. She hoped Sweet Cove didn't become a town that guests visited just because of weird happenings.

"The murders were both solved, however." Mr. Roberts finished his coffee.

Mrs. Roberts had more to share with the other people at the table. "Yesterday, when I stopped in at one of the stores in the center of Sweet Cove, I overheard...."

Her husband interrupted. "She eavesdropped."

The woman waved her hand dismissively at Mr. Roberts and continued with her story. "I heard two women talking about the bomb in that house. They seemed to be very knowledgeable about the town and the goings-on here."

Mr. Roberts piped up again. "That means they are gossips."

Mrs. Roberts leveled her eyes at her husband. "That's nonsense, my dear." She turned back to her audience. "They were discussing possible suspects, but didn't have anyone in particular in mind. They also said that the people who own the house with the bomb are in an assisted living facility and they have a son who is estranged from them. And, listen to this. Years ago, a man was beaten to death in the house right next door to the house with the bomb. Imagine that? Such strange doings right there on the very same street. Years apart, but nonetheless." Mrs. Roberts shuddered. "I wouldn't want to live on that street."

The tiny blonde hairs on Angie's arms stood up. She'd never heard that a murder took place just one street over from the Victorian. Lifting a platter from the buffet table, she smiled sweetly and turned slowly towards Mrs. Roberts. "Where did you say you heard the information?"

Mrs. Roberts seemed surprised that Angie was in the room. She blinked a few times before answering. "It's that store in the center of town.

It's called ... um, what is it?" She looked at her husband for a second before the name of store popped into her head. "It's the gift shop on the corner. "Spoiled and Loved." Do you know it?"

Angie nodded. "It's a great gift shop. Did the people you overheard work at the store?"

Mrs. Roberts tapped her index finger against her temple. "I think one of them works there. She's short, a bit stout, middle-aged, sandy colored hair."

Angie smiled. "She's the owner. A very nice woman. Can I get anyone more to eat?"

The guests shook their heads and murmured "no thank you."

As Angie carried two platters to the kitchen, she thought an afternoon visit to the gift store in the center of town might prove very helpful, but first she had to text Betty Hayes. Jenna and Angie thought it was imperative for Betty to consider that she might have been the intended target of the bomb and they wanted to talk to her about who might have motive.

Angie thought she'd better bring a very large notebook to list all the people who might bear a grudge against Betty.

CHAPTER 8

The *Spoiled and Loved* gift shop was housed in a Greek Revival style home near the corner of Main Street and West Street. The walkway leading to the front porch of the store was lined with pink and white impatiens. Huge containers of red and pink geraniums were placed on each step and window boxes full of pink and lavender flowers lined the porch railings.

The bell over the door of the store tinkled announcing Angie's arrival. Customers wandered the aisles, inspecting the merchandise on shelves and display cases. A table was set to the side of one of the rooms with samples of crackers and jams to try before purchasing. Angie casually browsed through the shop's many rooms keeping an eye out for the owner.

In the last room in the back of the house, Angie spotted Lola Winters stacking the shelves with candles and she went over to say hello.

"Some of my employees called in sick today, so

I'm doing it all." Lola shook her head. She knew Angie from dropping in to the bake shop for lattes and sweets. "You know what it's like to own a business." Lola bent to remove more candles from the delivery carton. "When are you re-opening the bake shop?"

"Early August, if the rest of the renovations go well." Angie picked up a scented jar candle and sniffed. "You heard about the house on Willow Street?"

Lola made a face. "Who would do such a stupid thing? A bomb? Why?"

Angie shrugged. "My sister and I were with Betty Hayes and the man who was looking at the house when we became suspicious and left the building."

"You were in there? Oh, my." Lola put her hand over her heart.

"It was a shock to think we came so close to ... well, you know."

"What a world." Lola lifted more candles from the box and moved to the next shelf.

"Have you heard any talk about who might have put the bomb in the house?"

"Not really. Mostly gossip. People say someone was living in the house secretly and when it went up for sale the guy put a bomb in there."

"You think it's true?" Angie handed a few boxes of candles to Lola.

"Who knows? You heard the owners are in

assisted living? They have a son, but they don't talk to each other."

"I wonder why they don't get along."

"I met the couple a few times. I didn't like the man. He seemed like a hard one. One of those big businessmen who think everyone should bow down before them. People told me he was demanding, rigid. Maybe he was too hard on the son."

"What was the wife like?"

"She was lovely. Nice conversationalist. Very pretty woman." Lola sighed. "What's wrong with Willow Street, anyway? You heard there was a murder there a long time ago? In the house right next door to the house with the bomb. You probably weren't even born when it happened."

"Someone mentioned it to me. I'd never heard anything about it before."

"Who'd want to live over there with the bad stuff that's happened? Makes a person think there's a curse on that street."

A shudder ran down Angie's spine. "It's just a coincidence." She had to shake herself to throw off a sense of unease that tried to cling to her. Something about the conversation with Lola made her feel nervous, but she couldn't understand why.

Angie's phone buzzed. It was a text from Betty Hayes replying to Angie's request to meet. *I can meet you in an hour at the main office, but I can't stay long.*

"I need to get home." She said goodbye to Lola

and headed to the front of the store. As Angie was leaving the candle room, Lola called to her. "Stay safe."

The words skittered over her skin and made her shiver.

***

Jenna and Angie opened the door to Sweet Cove Realty and glanced around for Betty. The receptionist, a middle-aged, short blonde in a long skirt saw the girls come in and hurried over to them.

"Betty's on the phone. Come sit here." She smiled and led them to a round table near the front windows. "She'll be right over. Can I get you something? Tea, coffee, water?"

The sisters thanked the woman, but declined the beverages.

"Betty won't take this seriously." Jenna looked around the office which was tastefully decorated with warm lighting and comfortable furniture. The space gave the impression of a modern, efficient, and successful business.

Angie sighed. "Maybe we can drag a list of possible suspects out of her. We can tell Chief Martin, and even if Betty doesn't want to be careful, at least the rest of us can keep an eye out."

"Mr. Finch is worried about her."

"He might have good reason to be." Angie

spotted Betty coming towards them. "Here she comes."

Betty pulled out one of the plush chairs and plopped onto it. She nodded. "Jenna. Angie." She blew out a long breath. "First time I've sat down today." She checked her phone. "I only have a few minutes. What's the chit chat about?" She leaned back with her phone in her lap and rested her hands on the arms of the chair. Betty saw the expression of seriousness on the girls' faces. "Oh, I know, you want to warn me that I might be in danger. Victor told me." She batted the air with her hand. "He's a worry-wart. A lovable one, though. But really, girls, you're making a mountain out of a molehill."

Jenna's jaw dropped. "There was a bomb. We could have been killed in that house."

"But we weren't." Betty glanced at her phone again.

"Somebody planted a bomb in the house." Angie leaned forward. "Someone, *multiple people* could have been killed because of it. We have a responsibility to consider who could have put the bomb in there. Who's to say the perpetrator won't make another attempt."

Betty rubbed her temple. "It could be anyone."

"It could be, but let's narrow it down." Jenna pulled a pad and pen from her bag. "Let's talk about people who may bear a grudge against you."

Betty looked with annoyance at the pad of paper.

Angie tried a different tack. "If you don't think it's necessary to take steps to protect yourself, think of Mr. Finch's safety. You're together quite often. I'm sure you don't want to put him at any risk."

"Oh, for heaven's sake." Betty frowned. "What do you want to know?"

"Is there anyone who holds a grudge against you or was anyone ever angry with you over a business dealing?" Jenna hoped Betty would give the question some thought before dismissing the notion.

Betty squirmed in her seat. "There's a huge list."

"Well, how about just the ones who were the angriest?" Angie suggested.

"I can't really think of anyone who stands out." Betty tapped her polished nails on the table.

The blonde receptionist had been hovering near the table a few feet away speaking with one of the other Realtors. She moved with purpose and stepped over to the table where Betty and the girls were sitting. "If you won't say anything, then I will."

Angie's eyes were wide. "Sit with us."

"Louisa...." Betty spoke sternly.

"I don't care if you scold me," Louisa said. "You need to tell them about Mitchell Watson."

The sisters noticed a fleeting crack in Betty's armor.

"Who is he?" Angie asked.

Betty's cheeks were red. "He is a very annoying

man."

"Tell them." Louisa urged. "Or I will."

Betty squirmed in her seat. "I had business dealings with Mr. Watson. Things didn't go well. He became enraged."

Louisa's face was pinched. "He stalked Betty."

Jenna's and Angie's eyebrows shot up.

"However." Betty scowled. "He has stopped."

"The name Mitchell Watson sounds familiar." Angie pondered where she'd heard it. "Isn't he a land developer?"

"Yes, he is." Betty's entire face was cherry red.

"What got him so upset?" Jenna wrote the man's name on the pad.

"I listed land for sale over in the next town." Betty made eye contact with Angie. "Several parties were interested, including your boyfriend and his brother."

Angie wanted to say that Josh Williams wasn't her boyfriend, but then she wondered if he was. He wasn't in Sweet Cove very much so she wasn't sure how to categorize their relationship. Before she could decide what to say, Betty had moved on.

"Mitchell Watson thought I cut him out of the deal in favor of the Williams brothers. I did not. The offer the Williams' made was superior. Watson was a sore loser." Betty harrumphed.

"He was enraged," Louisa said. "He'd show up here at odd hours and just stare at the building. He went to Betty's house and would do the same, just stare at the home office attached to the side of her house. He was a nuisance. We reported him to the police. But these are public streets and there isn't any law against standing on the sidewalk. No matter how intimidating someone may be." The receptionist shook her head. "I've worked for Betty for thirty years. Sometimes you lose out on a property. It's the nature of the beast. If Watson can't handle it, he should be in another line of work."

"What made him stop harassing you?" Jenna asked.

"Who knows?" Betty fanned herself with one of the papers from the table. It was clear that the episode with Watson had unnerved her. "It just stopped."

"When did he stop?" Angie questioned.

"Just recently. I need a glass of water." Betty looked around.

The man at the next table got up. "I'll get it for you."

"How recently?" Jenna shared a look with her sister. *Did Watson stop his harassment because he came up with a way to hurt Betty?*

Betty looked at her receptionist. "What would you say? He stopped the stalking, what ... about ten days or so ago?"

Louisa nodded. "That's about right. We heard he went off to Las Vegas for some land deal. He better not come back."

The other Realtor brought the glass of water to the table and Betty grabbed it and gulped. Louisa made introductions. "This is one of our new Realtors, Brian Hudson."

Hudson shook hands with the girls. "You were with Betty on the day the bomb was found?"

Angie and Jenna were slightly surprised that people knew they were in the Willow Street house that day.

Angie nodded. "It was a shock. It still is."

"It was a shock to me as well." Hudson's facial muscles tensed.

Louisa said, "Brian lives in the house next door."

Angie's eyebrows shot up. "Next door?" *In the house where the murder took place?*

Hudson blew out a breath. "If that bomb went off, it would have taken my house out with it." He gave a shoulder shrug. "Of course, that would be inconsequential if there was loss of life."

Angie leaned forward. "Did you ever notice anyone around the house? There's some gossip that someone was living there without permission."

"No. I never noticed anybody around the place. Living next door to an unoccupied building isn't the best thing. Kids can get in there, homeless. A lot of damage could be done. I kept an eye out for anything like that."

Jenna noted, "It must have taken some time to get the bomb in there and rig it up. It couldn't be set up that quickly, could it?"

"It really wouldn't take that long to set it up. It must have been done when I was at work, or asleep. I'm away from home a lot. I don't keep regular hours."

Angie said, "That would have made it more difficult to plant the bomb since the perpetrator wouldn't know when you'd actually be home. It would be easier to put the bomb in the house if a neighbor had a regular routine."

Hudson checked the time. "Well, it's over and done with now. The bomb has been dismantled and taken away." He excused himself. "I need to see a client. Nice to meet you."

Angie didn't think the danger was over just because the bomb had been discovered and removed. Someone who went to that much trouble to plant a bomb probably wouldn't just sit back and say 'oh well.'

Jenna kept her voice low. "Does Mr. Hudson know that a murder was committed in his house?"

"Yes, he does." Betty stood up. "I have an appointment, as well. I'll see you girls later."

Just as the girls were about to get up from their seats, Louisa looked over her shoulder and then turned back to them. "It was Brian's father."

Angie gave the receptionist a questioning look.

Louisa tilted her head towards Brian Hudson who was standing at his desk hurriedly gathering up some papers for his appointment. "The man who was murdered years ago, it was Brian's father."

CHAPTER 9

"His father?" Jenna eyes bugged out. "He lives in the same house where his father was murdered?"

"Brian lived in the house on Willow Street with his mom and dad. He was only fourteen years old when his father was killed."

"He and his mom stayed there after the father was killed?" Angie couldn't believe that Brian's mother would remain in the house where her husband had been murdered.

Louisa shook her head. "No. They left town almost immediately. They moved to North Carolina where Brian's mother had a sister. Brian didn't know that his mother had kept the Willow Street house and that she'd been renting it out all that time. He only found out six months ago, when his mother died and he inherited the house. He had just gotten divorced so he decided to move back to Sweet Cove."

"I'm not sure I would have moved back, not into the same house, anyway." The corners of Jenna's mouth turned down.

"I guess time passes." Angie's eyes were sad. "Maybe people forget the worst parts of things."

"I don't think Brian could ever forget." Louisa reached for the empty glass on the table that Betty had left behind. "He was the one who found his father's body."

***

Angie and Jenna walked along the sidewalk through the center of town.

"How awful." Angie slowly shook her head. "A fourteen-year-old boy found his father murdered in their own house. I can't even fathom it."

"It's amazing he's willing to return to the house at all, never mind actually live in it," Jenna said. "He must be focusing on the good times he had there with his parents and blocking out the nightmare of finding his murdered father."

Angie's phone buzzed. A worried look passed over her face. "It's Chief Martin. He has Mr. Cook, the father, at the police station. He wants to know if we can come right over there."

"Maybe Courtney's right." Jenna pushed her long braid over her shoulder. "Maybe Chief Martin *should* make us deputies."

The girls hurried the several blocks to the station. Chief Martin was waiting for them in the lobby.

"Mr. Chip Cook, the father, arrived a little while

ago." He cocked his head towards the other side of the lobby where a burly man with tattoos inked into both forearms sat reading a magazine. "That's Cook's personal assistant and driver." The chief raised his eyebrows. "He drove him here to Sweet Cove. I didn't tell the son that his father is in town." The chief led the girls down the hallway to the conference room. "This guy impresses me as someone who gets his way. He says he still works. I don't think he would've moved to assisted living if the wife didn't need the care. I won't say any more. See what you think. Same drill as the last time."

Jenna wasn't with them the last time they did an interview, so she gave Angie a questioning look.

"Just follow along." Angie entered the room with her sister right behind her.

An older man with a full head of snow white hair sat at the table. He stood up when the girls came in. He wore light gray slacks, a starched white shirt, and a dark gray linen jacket. Cook had wide shoulders. He looked trim and robust, not like someone who needed to be residing in an assisted living facility. Something about his manner and bearing made Angie wary.

The chief introduced the girls using Courtney's previous description of criminal justice consultants.

"Criminal justice consultants? What does that mean?" Cook looked down his nose at the sisters.

"It means...." Jenna gave the man a look devoid of emotion. "That we solve crimes."

79

Angie had to suppress a smile. Jenna was as good as Courtney at deflecting attempted intimidation.

Cook made a face as if Jenna's comment was distasteful to him. "You don't look like police officers."

They all took seats. The chief thanked Cook for coming to Sweet Cove on such short notice.

"Well, unfortunately, my house had a bomb in it, so I'm here. I'm always on the move. I travel around the state on business. We were heading back to Boston. This little detour happened to be convenient."

Angie wondered if Mr. Cook would have refused the chief's request to meet if it hadn't been convenient for him.

"You have business in Boston?" Chief Martin asked.

"I live in Boston." Cook adjusted the cuff of his shirt.

"I thought you lived in Wayland. At the assisted living place."

Cook's eyes narrowed. "I have a condo in Boston. That's where I spend most of my time. I have a cottage at the assisted living community. I use it when I visit my wife. It's not my permanent residence."

"Well, I misunderstood." The chief looked at the paperwork spread in front of him. He pushed two papers across the table. "You filled these in to sell your house on Willow Street?"

Cook took a quick look at the forms. "I did."

"You listed your son as the second contact."

Cook scowled. "My *son* and I don't get along. I've written him out of my life. I don't even consider that I ever had a son. I thought I was required to write down a next of kin. Otherwise, I wouldn't have listed him."

Angie's dislike of this man was growing with every word he uttered.

The chief placed the forms back into the folder. "May I ask the nature of your estrangement from your son?"

"No, you may not." Cook gave a slight shoulder shrug. "It has nothing to do with the bomb in the Willow Street house, if that's what you're thinking. It's more of a *personality conflict*." He gave a forced smile.

Jenna didn't like the arrogant man and she gave Angie a quick glance. Cook spotted their momentary exchange. "Is there a problem?"

"Not with us." Jenna's voice even and calm. *But there is with you.* She kept that thought to her self.

The chief asked, "Do you have any ideas about who might have planted a bomb in your home? Is there a disgruntled employee, an angry client, a colleague, someone who may have resented you?"

Cook chortled. "There would be quite a few names on a list like that."

Chief Martin scrutinized the man sitting across

the table from him. "We're trying to solve a crime, a crime that took place on your property. We'd appreciate your assistance."

"I'm not a member of law enforcement. Why don't you use your resources?" Cook checked the time on the heavy gold watch attached to his wrist. "Your time is up. I must move on to my next appointment." He stood. "I'd like to get that house sold and off my hands before another bomb gets put in there." He made eye contact with the three people across from him. "Any takers?"

No one replied.

Cook guffawed. "I thought not." He strode out of the room and pulled the door shut behind him with a bang that caused Angie to jump.

"What an obnoxious jerk." Angie stood up and rubbed her shoulders to ease the tension that had built up in her muscles during the interview.

Jenna was steaming. "What is his problem? You're trying to protect his asset and all he does is mock us and take off."

"We might wonder why he bothered to stop here at all." The chief raised an eyebrow.

Angie picked up on the chief's tone. "What are you getting at?"

"Why would he bother to come to the police station, with his thug driver, stay for a few minutes, and tell us basically nothing. And in a mocking tone, I might add." Chief Martin gathered the papers on the table and put them all back into the folder. "I suppose the reason could be nothing more than that the man is an arrogant jerk."

A thrumming of anxiety pulsed through Angie's veins for a few moments and then was gone, leaving her with a sickening sense of unease. "I feel something. Anxiety. That something isn't right."

Jenna eyed her sister. "Are you left with those feelings because Mr. Cook is a rude jerk or because of something else?"

Angie's forehead creased as she puzzled over the sensations. "I think it's more than him being a jerk. But I don't know why or what I'm picking up on."

Chief Martin sighed and leaned back in his chair. "Mr. Cook was clearly sending us a message. What that message was supposed to be, I couldn't make out."

"What happened with the inspector this morning? Did Charlie Cook meet you at the house?" Jenna asked.

"The meeting was postponed. The inspector contacted me at the last minute." The chief looked up at the wall clock. "We're meeting in two hours." He stacked the folders on top of each other and stood up. "Why don't you join us? Can you get away?"

A wave of nervousness flashed through Angie's veins from thinking of returning to the Willow Street house. She took a quick look at her sister to gauge her reaction and then looked at the chief. "Are you sure the house is safe?" she asked in a small voice.

"You can wait outside, if you like. You don't need to go in. I thought it might be helpful to have you two around when Charlie Cook is there."

Angie's eyes went wide. "Oh. I forgot to tell you." She proceeded to inform the chief that she saw Cook skulking around the Willow Street house late at night.

"Hmm." Chief Martin stroked his chin. "It could be that he just got an urge to go look around his family's house. He said he hadn't been there in a long time. Maybe he preferred to return to it in private?"

"Could be." Jenna nodded, thinking about Cook and his motives.

"But he told us he had no ties to the place. That he barely spent any time there," Angie said.

"Some people lie," Jenna noted with a frown.

Angie's eyes brightened with an idea. "We should talk to Brian Hudson. Ask what he knows about the Cook family." She looked at the chief. "Hudson lives next door to the Cook's house. He lived there when he was a young boy. You know he was the one who found his father's murdered body?"

Chief Martin nodded. "I know he moved back here recently. He's working at Betty's real estate office. Hard to fathom wanting to live in that house again." He sighed. "So many questions to answer." He looked hopefully at the girls. "Will I see you this afternoon?"

Jenna and Angie exchanged a glance and then answered together. "We'll be there."

CHAPTER 10

Angie and Jenna sat at the desks in the jewelry room. Jenna placed gemstones and silver findings onto a felt mat. She moved some around and then replaced them with different stones. When she was happy with the design, she slid the mat to Angie who then began the construction of the pieces into the final product.

Euclid and Circe sat next to Ellie on the sofa. She stroked the cats' soft fur while she listened to Angie and Jenna take turns telling about their morning and what they had learned including Betty's stalker, that Brian Hudson had found his murdered father's body, that Brian returned to Sweet Cove to live in the house that had been the scene of the crime, and about meeting the older Mr. Cook and that he had an obnoxious personality.

"I guess you didn't have a very productive morning as far as gathering information," Ellie teased. She pulled some of her hair over her shoulder and absent-mindedly worried the ends with her fingers. "Are all small towns like this?

Crazy goings-on, secret land deals, murders." She shivered.

"This stuff goes on everywhere." Jenna spoke without looking up from her work. "You just hear more about it in small towns because people know each other."

Angie peeked at Ellie. "Will you come with us when we go over to Willow Street to meet Chief Martin this afternoon?"

Ellie didn't answer right away which made Angie turn her head to see if her sister had heard the question. Ellie looked deep in thought as she slid her hand over the black cat's fur.

"Ellie?"

She blinked and lifted her face. "I was thinking. Maybe you should take the cats with you when you go over to Willow Street."

Euclid and Circe trilled at the idea.

Angie and Jenna swiveled their chairs towards the sofa where Ellie was sitting.

Ellie said, "The cats have been helpful before. They seem to be able to sense a person's character."

"I think they can do more than that," Jenna muttered. She had no idea what the cats were capable of and she would never doubt their ability to figure things out.

"I think that's a good idea to bring the cats." Angie held a gemstone in one hand and the end of the beading wire in her other hand. "But we might be preoccupied when we're there. Would you come along and keep an eye on them? You know, in case a dog comes by or whatever."

Ellie's posture seemed to shrink. Her mouth turned down in a frown. "I'm afraid to go over there." Her voice was tiny.

"It's daylight." Jenna leaned over her desk moving stones around to create a new design using just the right colors. "We'll be together. Chief Martin will be there. What could happen?"

Angie and Ellie turned to their sister. Neither one wanted to verbalize what had come very close to happening, but finally Ellie said, "Well, for one thing, the house could blow up."

***

The unusual procession made its way through the Victorian's backyard with Jenna in the lead, followed by Euclid, Circe, and Ellie, and Angie taking up the rear. They headed for the woods that lined the back of the property and squeezed through the grove of bushes, shrubs, and trees, emerging onto the weedy lawn of the Colonial-style house on Willow Street.

The girls were able to convince Ellie to accompany them to the house inspection so that she could keep an eye on the cats. Angie pointed out that if the Willow Street house did explode, there would be so much fire power unleashed that Ellie probably wasn't that much safer being inside the Victorian. Ellie's face blanched at the remark, but she decided that if Angie was right, then she might as well help her sisters by watching over the cats.

Brian Hudson's car, with *Sweet Cove Realty* written on the passenger side door, was parked at the curb. Hudson, Chief Martin, and the inspector were heading up the walkway towards the house. The chief waved to the girls. Charlie Cook was standing on the front lawn staring at the house with his arms crossed over his chest. He gave a cursory nod to the three men.

There was a black sedan parked in the driveway. Angie thought the car looked familiar and as she was trying to place where she had seen it, the front door of the house opened and the older Mr. Cook and his burly assistant stepped out.

"Uh, oh." Angie looked to Charlie Cook for his reaction to seeing his father emerge from the house.

"This should be interesting." Jenna put her hands in the pockets of her shorts. "Maybe we should stay right here and watch the fireworks."

"Let's move closer." Angie glanced at the cats. "I want to hear what everyone is saying."

Charlie and his father scowled at each other. Charlie didn't move from his spot on the lawn. The father pulled himself up to full height, turned away from his son, and walked towards Chief Martin.

"Chief." The older Cook gave a cursory nod.

"I didn't know you were coming to the house."

Chief Martin's face was serious. He was about to say more, but Cook cut him off.

"It is my house. I can enter whenever I like."

The personal assistant had a toothpick in his mouth and he moved it around from side to side. He stood back a few yards behind his boss.

Chief Martin narrowed his eyes. "It was recently the scene of a crime. The house is about to be fully inspected...." Again he was cut off by Cook.

"Wasn't it inspected previously?" Cook checked his watch with a bored expression on his face.

"It was inspected, yes, but we have an expert here from Boston to go through the place one more time. For safety sake."

The inspector spoke. "Explosive devices, incendiary devices ... they can be well hidden by people who know what they're doing. A second check-through is prudent in situations like this."

"Fine." Cook gave the sisters a quick look. He noticed Ellie standing beside Angie and Jenna and he cracked a sour smile. "Another criminal justice consultant? It takes three of you to figure things out?" Cook looked down at the cats sitting at the girls' feet. "I see you brought your sidekicks to help you."

Euclid arched his back and hissed. Circe's green eyes glowed and she growled low in her throat.

Cook turned to Chief Martin. "Don't you have anything better to spend the department's money on besides three *consultants* and two cats?"

The personal assistant chuckled. The sisters scowled at the idiot.

Brian Hudson stepped forward and extended his hand. "Hello, Mr. Cook. I'm Brian Hudson." When Cook didn't reciprocate, the Realtor quickly dropped his hand.

"Who are *you*?" The corners of Cook's mouth turned down.

"I'm the Realtor and...." Brian began.

Cook sneered. "I didn't hire you."

"Betty Hayes couldn't make the afternoon appointment with the inspector so I stepped in. We all work together at Ms. Hayes' real estate office."

"Do you know what you're doing? Do you know the neighborhood?" Cook demanded.

Angie noticed that Charlie had quietly come up to stand beside her.

Charlie glared at his father. He didn't make any attempt to greet the older man, but said, "I think he knows the neighborhood pretty well since he lives next door. Don't you recognize him? It's Brian Hudson. John Hudson's son."

Cook's eyes narrowed. His face became flushed. "I don't care who he is." He started towards his car, his assistant lumbering after him. As he walked, Cook shot a look at Brian Hudson. "Just sell this dump of a house."

Everyone stood in awkward silence watching Cook head to his car.

Euclid arched his back and let out an enormous

hiss.

"Exactly." Ellie agreed with the huge orange cat.

"What an awful man." When Jenna realized that Charlie heard her criticism, she quickly apologized.

Charlie shrugged. "Don't apologize. He is who he is. Your comment is dead on."

The chief, Brian Hudson, and the inspector went inside the house to begin their inspection of the premises.

Thinking Angie was part of law enforcement, Charlie asked, "Aren't you going with them?"

For a second, Angie didn't understand why she'd be expected to go inside with the chief and a bomb expert, but then she remembered that she and Courtney had told Charlie they were assistants to the Sweet Cove Police department. "No. It's better with fewer people." She wished she hadn't told a lie about her role, but then she wondered how she would possibly explain why she was involved. She could just imagine telling Charlie that she could "feel" things sometimes, and then seeing the horrified look on his face.

"We're heading home." Jenna touched Angie's arm. "You coming?"

"I'll be right there."

"We'll take the cats." Jenna, Ellie, and Circe headed for the path through the woods to the Victorian.

Euclid scowled at Charlie, gave a hiss and arched his back before turning to follow the others, his huge orange plume in the air.

"What's wrong with the cat?" Charlie asked.

Angie watched Euclid parade away to the tree line, wondering about his response to Charlie Cook. "That's a very good question." She turned her attention back to the house. "I hope they don't find anything else in there."

She heard Charlie let out a long sigh.

Angie asked, "You never spent much time here?"

"A few weekends here and there."

"Do you have any attachment to the place?"

"Really? No. Other families who have beach houses must have fond memories of spending time together at the seashore, having cookouts, being with friends. Not me. Sweet Cove is a nice town. It could have been fun." He paused. "If I'd been part of another family."

Angie could practically touch the sadness coming off of the man. It made her heart heavy, but then she thought of Euclid's reaction to Charlie and decided to mention that she'd seen him walking around the house in the dark. "I was in the backyard of the Victorian the other night. I saw you come through the woods from here."

Charlie's eyes widened in surprise and he moved his hand nervously over his hair, but quickly caught himself and tempered his response. He shoved his hands into the pockets of his chinos. "I couldn't relax that night. I went outside on the porch and sat in one of the rocking chairs for a while. Then I realized that my parents' house was on the other side of the woods. I got the urge to go look around." He shrugged.

Angie nodded and gave a little smile. "I'm going to head home. Are you going back to New Hampshire tonight?"

"No, I've booked a few more nights at the B and B. I figure I'll stick around a little while and see what happens with the house."

Angie told Charlie she'd see him later and headed for the woods. She thought over Charlie's explanation of why he was in the backyard of his parents' place late at night.

If you just got the urge to go look around the house while you were sitting on the front porch, why did you have a flashlight with you?

CHAPTER 11

When Angie pushed through the shrubs into her backyard, she saw her sisters and Mr. Finch talking together by the carriage house and she hurried over to them.

"We're just bringing Courtney and Mr. Finch up to speed on what's been going on." Jenna reached down to scratch Euclid's cheek. Circe sat in one of the patio chairs.

Angie told them what Charlie Cook said about being in his parents' backyard the other night. She voiced her skepticism over his explanation. "He had a flashlight. Wouldn't that indicate he had other plans besides just sitting on the porch?"

"I think you're right." Courtney looked towards the woods.

"And Euclid gave Charlie a scowl and a hiss just as he left to come home," Angie said.

The three sisters and Finch looked down at the orange cat.

Finch said, "He must sense something. It will take time to determine what Euclid doesn't like about Mr. Charlie Cook."

"Cook will be around for a few more days so maybe we can figure it out." Ellie reached for the knob on the door of the carriage house and opened it. "We were just going up to Mr. Finch's apartment."

"I thought you should see something." Finch leaned on his cane and politely held back so the girls could climb the stairs ahead of him to the second floor.

"I haven't seen the apartment since you moved in." Angie stepped into the combination living-dining room. She smiled when she saw the colorful abstract painting hanging above the desk. It had been a gift to Mr. Finch from his Swedish grandmother. Finch's terrible brother stole the painting from him when they were young men and the beautiful painting had recently been recovered and returned to Mr. Finch after fifty years in his brother's possession.

"Now I have somewhere to display it." Mr. Finch stood tall and happy gazing at the painting on his wall.

Angie touched his arm. "I'm very glad that the painting is back where it belongs." Her eyes got misty and she brushed at them with her hand. She swallowed. "What did you want to show us?"

Finch gestured to one of the bedrooms at the rear of the apartment. "I think you'll find this interesting in light of the events of the past days."

The girls, the two cats, and Finch went into the bedroom.

"I noticed the view from the window." Finch pointed. "I thought it might be useful at times."

Courtney moved to the window and peered out. "Wow. What a great view." She turned around with an impish grin. "This could be very handy."

The apartment window overlooked the tree line between the Victorian and Cook's Colonial. It also afforded a splendid view of Brian Hudson's house and yard.

Mr. Finch moved closer to the window. "Not that any of us wish to become Peeping Toms, but due to the dangerous situation thrust upon us by the unfortunate presence of a bomb very close to our home, well, in order to maintain our safety, we must use our resources."

"Absolutely right." Ellie agreed with Mr. Finch's statement. She leaned over her sister's shoulder to admire the view. "Good thing the carriage house was built with so much height. We can see right over the treetops."

Jenna asked Courtney and Finch, "Are you home for dinner or do you have to get back to the candy store?"

"We're home for dinner, and then I'm going back to the store for part of the evening," Courtney said. "Mr. Finch and I are going to take turns checking the store after dinner each night."

"That way," Finch winked, "we each have the

opportunity to engage in a social life."

Angie raised one eyebrow. She had a mischievous grin on her face. "Which reminds me...." She looked straight at her youngest sister. "We haven't had a chance to hear about Rufus Fudge."

"You mean tease her about Mr. Fudge." Jenna gave Courtney a playful smile.

"I'm not sure I have any idea what you're talking about." Courtney kept her face blank, but the sisters could see that she was making a mighty effort to suppress a smile. "I'm going back to the Victorian to start dinner." She left the apartment.

Hearing the word "dinner" caused the cats to chase after her.

"She's not getting away that easy." Jenna was the next one to leave the apartment.

Angie smiled at Ellie and Mr. Finch. "The Rufus Fudge interrogation begins." They started down the staircase together.

"Where'd he get a name like 'Rufus Fudge'anyway?" Ellie pondered.

"Perhaps from his parents," Mr. Finch joked.

The sisters chuckled as the three of them made their way across the walkway to the back door of the house.

***

The rear yard of the Victorian had three separate

98

areas where the Roseland sisters and the bed and breakfast guests could relax. A stone patio was right off the back door of the house, and depending on the time of day, half the space was in the shade of a large tree and the other half was in the sun. On the side of the yard away from the carriage house, another stone patio sat beneath a white pergola. Climbing roses and clematis edged up the sides and top of the structure. A month ago, a craftsman recommended by Tom had completed a third patio with a circular stone fireplace in the center. Many of the B and B guests enjoyed gathering around the fire in the evenings with a cup of coffee or a glass of wine. Ellie had taken up gardening and she added more perennials and annuals to the flower beds edging the property.

Angie sat in one of the Adirondack chairs sipping some tea. She stared at the grove of trees at the back of her lawn that separated her house from the Cook's house. She had a few more minutes to sit before making the morning's deliveries of her baked goods to the local restaurants.

Euclid and Circe had settled in the opposite chair with their eyes glued to Angie.

"Why are you two staring at me like that?" She chuckled. "I don't have a fish in my back pocket you know."

The slap of the screen door caused Angie to turn towards the sound. Jenna headed her way with a cup of coffee in her hand.

"I thought you'd left already to do your deliveries." Jenna settled in the chair next to her sister. "What's with the cats? Do you have food out here?"

"They've been staring at me since I came out. I wish they'd stop."

"We need to talk about Courtney's birthday." Jenna blew on her hot coffee. "What should we plan?" It was tradition for the three older siblings to plan their baby sister's birthday celebration each year.

Angie said, "I've been thinking about that. I talked to Josh the other night when we went out. He suggested we have the party at the resort. He said we could have as many people as we want. He'll set aside some rooms for us to use for the day, in case people want to change out of swimsuits and we can use the kitchen in the suites to store food or cook."

"That sounds perfect." Jenna closed her eyes and tilted her face towards the sun. "We can swim at the beach, use the tennis courts, the pools. Courtney would love it."

"Should we invite friends up from Boston or just have a small group?"

Jenna thought about it. "I think if we invite the Boston crowd, it might get out of hand. Where would we draw the line? If we invite some and not others, people will feel badly."

"Let's just have us and Mr. Finch."

Jenna nodded. "And Tom and Josh and Jack Ford."

"Sounds like a plan." Angie finished her tea, set the cup on the arm of the chair, and extended her hands over her head in a big stretch. "I can't believe Courtney's going to be twenty-two."

"Time flies."

"Speaking of which, I better make those deliveries." Angie stood up.

"The keys to my car are on the kitchen pegboard." Jenna still nestled in the chair with her eyes closed.

Angie had junked her old car right after it nearly broke down when she was trying to rush back to the Victorian during the last mystery they'd solved. Since then, she'd been borrowing Jenna's sedan.

"Thanks." Angie headed for the back door.

"Don't worry. I'll send you the bill for my car rental."

CHAPTER 12

The late afternoon air hung heavy and hot on Angie's skin as she walked up Beach Street to the center of town. The forecast predicted a heat wave would settle over Sweet Cove with temperatures rising into the low nineties. Angie talked to Tom about installing more air conditioning units at the Victorian to keep the B and B guests cool and comfortable. She followed the brick sidewalks for a few blocks and then turned onto a side street lined with more shops. She continued for a few blocks until she reached the Sweet Cove Hair Design Salon.

"Hey, Angie." The receptionist greeted her and showed her to a seat in an empty booth where she could wait for her stylist.

Angie enjoyed coming to the salon to get her hair trimmed. She could relax in the chair and chat with the woman who had been cutting her hair for over a year.

Gloria bustled over. She was a petite woman in her sixties with light blonde hair and bright blue eyes. Her hair was cut short and feathered to frame her face, her nails were always manicured and polished, and her makeup was subtly, but skillfully applied to enhance her features. "What a day. I've been straight out. A client came a half-hour late and I sandwiched her in between two other customers."

She placed a plastic cape around Angie's neck and fluffed it over her shoulders. "I've finally caught up now and can take a breath." She ran a brush over Angie's honey blonde locks. "Don't you ever color this hair," Gloria clucked. "It's an absolute perfect shade of dark blonde."

Angie chuckled. Gloria said the same thing to her every time she came in. "I'm too lazy to have my hair colored. I don't want to be a slave to coming in all the time to have it done." She modified her statement. "I love you, Gloria. I just don't want to have an appointment every couple of weeks to tend my hair."

The two chatted about what was going on in their lives and then the conversation turned to town happenings.

"I can't believe the Willow Street bomb." Gloria shook her head. "What's wrong with people?"

Angie told the stylist that she and Jenna were in the house at the time the bomb was discovered.

"I can't believe it." Gloria lifted a section of hair and clipped a bit from the ends. "I've lived in this town my whole life. It's never been like this. It's just one bad thing after another recently."

Looking into the large mirror attached to the wall in front of the chair, Angie made eye contact with the stylist. "I heard a man was murdered on Willow Street a long time ago. It was John Hudson?"

Gloria shuddered. "That was an awful thing. I remember it like it was yesterday. Fear gripped the town when the news came out. I'd just opened the salon. I worked for years to save up money to open my own place. Even back then I did both men's and women's hair. Whenever I worked on a client, I would wonder if the person could be the killer. Silly, I know, but the mind tries to protect us, I suppose."

"Did you know the Hudson family? I met the son recently."

"He's the Realtor, Brian Hudson." Gloria leaned close. "I would never move back into the house where my father was killed." She held her scissors in mid-air. "No, I could not do that." She returned her attention to Angie's hair. "I didn't know the Hudsons. I didn't want to. I heard John Hudson was a rough man."

Angie was about to ask her what she meant by the comment when Gloria said, "I knew the woman who owns the bomb house."

Angie suppressed a smile at Gloria's name for the house on Willow Street. "I met her son recently, too."

"Did you?" Gloria used her foot to push on the bar at the base of the chair to raise it a few inches. "I used to do Elise Cook's hair when she was here for the summers."

Angie told Gloria that Mrs. Cook was in an assisted living facility due to having Alzheimer's disease.

"Oh, my, the ravages of time. I can't imagine her like that. Elise is a few years younger than I am. She's too young to have that disease. She was such a vivacious, vibrant woman."

"Was she?" Angie asked. "Her son described her differently. He said she was quiet, only had a few friends, preferred doing things like needlepoint."

Gloria scoffed. "That wasn't Elise Cook. Are you sure you met the right son?"

Angie stopped herself from nodding. She didn't want to cause a big chunk of her hair to get cut off. "Charlie Cook. His parents own the house on Willow Street."

"Well, then, the son sure didn't know his mother. Elise Cook was a firecracker. She had her son when she was only twenty. She told me she never wanted any kids at all. I always hoped she didn't make that sentiment plain to the boy." Gloria ran a comb through Angie's hair to check the length. "Anyway, the Cooks bought the house the year before the son left for college. Elise became a good customer ... for over twenty years. She loved to talk, told me just about everything." The salon owner lowered her voice. "Elise was a busy woman, if you know what I mean."

Angie crinkled her forehead. "How so?"

Gloria raised an eyebrow. "Busy. You know."

Angie looked blank.

"With men." Gloria gave a pointed look. "This was a perfect place for Elise to spend her summers, what with men coming and going all June, July, and August."

Angie's eyes almost fell from her head. "She was a prost...."

"No, no. Nothing like that." Gloria vigorously shook her head. "She did enjoy the company of men, however. She had a number of affairs in the years she summered here."

"She told you that stuff?"

"I'm a hairdresser, hon. Everyone tells me stuff."

"Did her husband know?" Angie asked. "I met him, too. He seems like a monster. I can't see him putting up with such things."

"I agree with that. Elise was very discreet. She told me that if Mr. Cook found out what she was up to, she'd be dead. She used to chuckle about that. She told me more than once, if she died suddenly, for me to suspect her husband."

Angie was dumbstruck. "If she suspected that her husband would react so violently to her affairs, why would she continue?"

"Elise struck me as an adventurous spirit.

Maybe it was a game she played, to outwit her husband. Anyway, he was probably doing the same thing, probably had affairs with plenty of women. Maybe Elise thought, what's good for the goose is good for the gander. She hated her husband, but he had the dollars and she wasn't leaving the money tree. Her words. It stuck in my head because I'd never met a woman so bold."

A flash of anxiety skittered over Angie's skin leaving her feeling tense and on edge. She couldn't reconcile the person Gloria described with the quiet, gentle person the son recounted. Something was off, but she couldn't quite see what it was or why there was such a discrepancy in perception from Gloria and Charlie Cook. Angie squeezed her hands together in her lap under the plastic salon cape. "Did she tell you who she was having affairs with?"

"My, no. That is where I drew the line. I didn't want to know the details, no names." Gloria huffed. "If Mr. Cook ever found out about Elise's encounters and he happened to come in here to question me, I wanted to be sure I couldn't answer him. It's for the best not to know some things."

"How could Charlie Cook be so mistaken about his mother's personality? I'm sure she hid her affairs from her son, but she must have been an outgoing and energetic woman from the way you describe her. Charlie painted a very different picture with his description."

"Maybe Elise was a very good actress?" Gloria suggested. "Maybe she played one part at home and another when she was out?"

"Or," Angie said, "Charlie is creating the mother he never had."

CHAPTER 13

Angie stood at the stove on the side of the kitchen that Tom had recently renovated for household use. The changes he made created a large kitchen that was delineated into two parts, personal and commercial, with one side for the family's use and the other side for cooking and baking for the B and B and for Angie's bake shop.

Courtney came into the room. She'd returned home from the candy store, showered, and changed into jean shorts and a pale yellow T-shirt. "What's cookin'?"

"Plenty." Angie sautéed onions and mushrooms in a pan with a bit of garlic. The aroma fluttered on the air and made the girls' mouths water. "Listen to this." She proceeded to tell her sisters what she'd learned at the hair salon about Charlie's mother, Elise Cook.

"Yikes." Courtney washed lettuce leaves in the sink. "It seems she led a double life."

Jenna sliced tomatoes, red peppers, and cucumbers at the granite counter next to Angie. "Is what Gloria told you accurate?"

"I don't see why not. She seemed to know Elise Cook fairly well." Angie added a little olive oil to the pan. "Is Mr. Finch coming home for dinner?"

"He's staying at the candy store," Courtney reported. "Betty is picking him up there at eight and they're going to the resort for dinner."

"I don't know how someone could lead two lives like that." Ellie was doing paperwork at the kitchen table. "How could she get away with it? How did her husband not know? Or did he choose to ignore it?"

"Mr. Cook didn't spend much time in Sweet Cove." Courtney pulled a large bowl from the cabinet to use for the salad. "Since he wasn't around, Elise didn't have to hide things from him."

"But what about when Cook did spend time here? Elise and her beau, or beaus, would have had to be very discreet," Ellie noted.

"I bet she didn't tell many people about her extracurricular activities." Angie removed the pan from the burner. "Maybe she only told Gloria."

"That would have been the safer thing to do." Jenna handed the chopped veggies to Courtney to add to the salad. "Elise is still alive so her horrid husband mustn't have ever discovered her busy schedule. He doesn't seem like the kind of man who would put up with his wife cheating on him."

The girls carried platters of food to the dining table and sat down to the feast just as the doorbell rang.

"Maybe it's one of the guests. They probably forgot the entry code and are locked out." Ellie got up to open the front door. The girls had Tom install a lock on the Victorian's front door with a key pad that would unlock the door when the correct code was punched in. Guests were always losing keys to the house, so having the keypad at the door eliminated the need to copy keys over and over and reduced the inconvenience of guests being locked out of the B and B.

Ellie opened the door to see a vaguely familiar face. It took her a second to place the man. "Oh, Mr. Hudson. Please, come in."

"Sorry to bother you." Brian Hudson saw everyone sitting around the dining table. "You're having dinner. I'll come back."

Angie stood up and walked into the foyer. She smiled at the Realtor. "What can we do for you?"

"I was hoping to have a chat with you." He looked unsure. "All of you."

Angie wondered what Hudson wanted to talk about. "Why don't you join us then? There's plenty of food. We always make too much. Have you eaten?"

"No. I just finished work. I don't want to impose." Hudson eyed the living room on the other side of the foyer. "I could just wait for you until you finish dinner." He looked back to the dining table. "It does smell delicious."

"Come and eat." Angie touched the man's arm and steered him to an empty chair at the table. "In this house, our motto is, the more the merrier. That includes people and food."

Hudson didn't put up any resistance.

Courtney grinned. "It has to be our motto since we live in a B and B with people and food all around."

Ellie went to the kitchen and returned with a place setting for Hudson. Jenna passed him the bottle of Merlot. When everyone was settled and their plates were full, Angie asked, "What did you want to talk to us about?"

Hudson cleared his throat. "I spoke with Betty Hayes. I also read the newspaper." He hesitated.

"Is something wrong?" Ellie sipped her wine.

"No." Hudson answered quickly. "Well, I guess there is."

The girls gave him time to gather his thoughts.

"Betty Hayes suggested I talk to you. I read about all of you in the newspaper."

Angie eyed him, afraid of where this was going.

Hudson continued. "I read an article about how the four of you solved two murders in town."

"Oh, no. That wasn't us, really. It was our two cats." Courtney reached for more salad.

Hudson chuckled. "I'd like to meet these animals."

Courtney pointed to the China cabinet where Euclid and Circe sat perched, listening to the conversation at the table. "They sort of prefer not to be referred to as animals."

The cats stared at Hudson with unfriendly gazes. Euclid hissed. Hudson lost his smile and swallowed. "Anyway. You probably heard that my father passed away about twenty-five years ago. He was murdered. Right in our house on Willow Street."

Angie placed her fork on her plate. "We heard about that just recently."

"My mother died six months ago. She left me the house. And, a letter."

"What sort of letter?" Ellie's face was starting to lose its color.

"As you know, the killer was never caught. My mother wrote me a letter urging me to investigate my father's death. She was full of remorse that she didn't press enough for the crime to be solved." He glanced around the table at the four sisters. "I have no idea where to start. I don't know anything about investigating a crime."

Angie had a sinking feeling in her stomach. She knew what Hudson was about to ask.

"Since you have experience, I wondered if...."

Courtney sat up with a smile on her face. "You want us to investigate for you? That's great."

Angie shot her sister a look and then turned her attention back to Hudson. "Why don't you speak with the police? I'm sure they could offer you more help than we can. Our involvement in those two murders you read about ... well, what we discovered, it was all sort of accidental. We didn't really figure things out."

Courtney looked crestfallen.

Jenna said, "What Angie means is that we probably wouldn't be any help and it would end in disappointment for you. The newspaper exaggerated about our abilities, I'm afraid."

"But you *were* involved in solving those two recent murders in Sweet Cove?" Hudson wasn't going to let go easily.

Courtney piped up. "Yes, we were."

"Well, that's good enough for me. If you can't find out anything about my father's murder, then I'm no worse off, am I?"

"Good point," Courtney said. She looked hopefully at her sisters.

"I don't think it's a good idea," Ellie muttered.

"Would you try?" Hudson's eyes were sad. "It would mean a lot to me."

Angie wished they hadn't opened the door when the bell rang. She knew she couldn't refuse after seeing the loss in Hudson's eyes. She was defeated.

"I guess we could look into it," Jenna said softly.

"When can we start?" Courtney's eyes shined.

The dinner dishes were cleared from the table. Tea and coffee were served. Ellie tried to linger in the kitchen, but Angie asked her to sit with them to talk about the murder. Ellie's hands were trembling when she sat down. Noticing her shaky fingers, she placed them in her lap.

"So." Angie took a deep breath. "I guess we should start at the beginning. What can you tell us about what happened?"

Brian Hudson clasped his hands together and put them on the table. He leaned over, his head hanging forward. "I was fourteen years old when it happened. My mother was making dinner and we were waiting for Dad to get home. He had to work late on Wednesdays. It was almost dark. I was watching some stupid cartoon or something on television." Hudson lifted his head and gazed off into the distance. "I thought I heard a noise in the garage. I went to see if Dad was just getting home or if the door got left open and maybe a raccoon got in."

He closed his eyes for several seconds. When he opened them, he continued. "The door to the garage was off the kitchen. I opened the door and stepped inside. Dad's car was parked there. I wondered where he was if his car was at home, but he wasn't. The garage door was open. I stepped into the garage and saw Dad on the floor." Hudson's face muscles tightened. "He was dead. There was no question about it. There was so much blood. Then I heard a strange high-pitched noise and wondered what it was. Turns out, it was me. The noise was coming out of me. I was screaming."

CHAPTER 14

Angie's heart clenched at the image of a fourteen-year-old boy standing in a garage screaming, staring at the body of his dead father. The dining room was deathly quiet for almost a full minute.

Angie took a quick glance up at the cats. The two sat at attention high up on the China cabinet, their eyes glued to Brian Hudson. Angie couldn't get a read on their emotions. Euclid made a tiny hiss.

Hudson let out a long, low sigh and slumped in his chair. "I can picture the scene like it was yesterday. The whole thing must be burned into my brain cells."

Ellie touched Hudson's arm. "I'm so sorry." Her eyes looked misty.

"Why don't I go make some more tea?" Jenna walked down the hall into the kitchen.

Angie stood up. "Would you like to continue to talk in the living room? It's more comfortable." She felt the need to move around and hoped that getting everyone to head to the living room chairs might dispel some of the tension and emotion they were all experiencing. Ellie and Courtney carried their coffee and tea mugs into the other room.

"Could I have another glass of wine?" Hudson asked.

Angie nodded and passed him the wine bottle. Hudson refreshed his glass and headed into the living room to sit in one of the chairs next to the sofa. Angie looked up for the cats. She wanted to encourage them to come to the other room, but they had already leaped from the China cabinet and were padding across the wood floor of the foyer.

Jenna returned carrying a tray with a full teapot, a fresh pot of cream, some dessert plates and a blackberry and raspberry cream cheese Danish roll that Angie had baked in the afternoon. Although it was intended for tomorrow morning's guests' breakfast buffet, Jenna thought that sweets always made people feel better. She sliced the Danish and passed the plates around. Courtney lifted the teapot and filled some of the mugs.

After the five of them had a few sips of wine or tea and several bites of the treat, Angie questioned Brian Hudson. "You know Charlie Cook?"

"Sure, the Cooks lived next door to us. Charlie wasn't around much. He was a few years older than me. A couple of times we shot some hoops in the driveway, but really, we didn't have much interaction."

"How about your parents? Were they friendly

with the Cooks?"

"Just to wave hello. To my knowledge, the dads never spoke. Mr. Cook was rarely around. Our moms didn't have much in common, I guess. We never socialized."

Jenna asked, "The evening you found your dad. Were the Cooks at home? Did they come over to help?"

Hudson looked across the room, thinking. "I don't remember. The police came. An ambulance came. Some neighbors were standing around outside watching." He shook his head. "I don't remember seeing any of the Cooks. They could have been around though. I just don't remember."

"That's understandable." Courtney offered him another piece of Danish.

"You mentioned your mother left you a letter with her will. Could we see it sometime?" Angie asked.

"Sure. I have it at home."

"Could we come by the house?" Jenna asked. "Take a look around, see the garage?"

Hudson looked surprised. "Sure, if you think it would be helpful."

Courtney placed her empty mug on the coffee table. "Can you tell us about your dad? What he did for work, who his friends were, did he have hobbies?"

Hudson leaned back in his chair. "Dad worked

at an auto body shop. He loved cars, loved working on them. Our house used to belong to my mom's family. She inherited it when her parents passed away. We moved to Sweet Cove when I was twelve. People would say Dad was kind of rough around the edges. He had very traditional ideas about men and women ... men should work, women should take care of the family."

"So your mother didn't work outside the home?" Angie asked.

"No, she was a stay-at-home mom. When we moved to North Carolina, she got a job working as a receptionist in a dentist's office."

"Did your dad have friends in the area?" Jenna questioned.

Hudson shook his head. "Once in a while, he'd go to a ballgame or out for a few beers with the guys he worked with, but mostly he worked and came home. Sometimes, he'd go fishing."

"What was the name of the auto body shop he worked at?" Jenna asked.

Hudson thought for a second. "It was in the next town over, the West Cove Garage."

Courtney asked, "Were you and your dad close? Did you do things together?"

"I wouldn't say we were close. We didn't do things together like some sons and dads, we didn't have conversations. We were just a normal family."

Angie didn't want to ask the next question, but if Hudson wanted help trying to find out who his father's killer was, she had to bring it up. "Do you have any idea who might have killed your father? Did he have a run-in with anyone? Get into a fight with someone?"

Hudson shrugged. "Not to my knowledge. But I was just a normal kid. I went to school, hung out, rode bikes, watched television. I didn't pay attention to what my parents were doing."

Jenna asked, "Are any of the kids you hung around with still in the area?"

"I don't know. I don't think so. I didn't have a lot of friends. I didn't grow up here and we moved away right after my dad died."

"How about neighbors?" Courtney questioned. "Are there any people still living on the street who were around at the time you and your parents lived in the house?"

Hudson took a swallow of his wine. "The Cooks still own their house. Not sure about anyone else. The house across the street is rented out to different families in the summer." He rubbed his face. "I work a lot. I hire someone to do the lawn. I'm not outside much so I don't meet the neighbors."

Angie broached another difficult subject. "It must be very hard to live in the house, what with the bad memories. What made you decide to move back to town?"

"When I was growing up, I didn't even know that my mom still owned the house. She left me the letter when she died. I suppose I was curious. I wanted to follow her wishes to try to find my father's killer." He drained his glass and was quiet for a minute. "I guess I should be going. I'll check my calendar. We can arrange a time for you to come to the house and look around, see the letter."

Hudson and Angie exchanged phone numbers, the girls walked the man to the door, and then the four sisters went to the family room at the back of the house to sit and talk.

"What do you think?" Ellie had been silent throughout the discussion with Hudson.

"I think it's going to be very difficult to find a killer from twenty-five years ago." Jenna plopped on the sofa. Circe curled up next to her.

"There isn't a lot to go on." Courtney sat in the chair next to Euclid. "Hudson doesn't know his father's friends, his mother is dead, and the neighbors are gone. Who is there to interview?"

Angie sighed. "I guess we can look at the letter his mom left him and take a look at the garage attached to the house. We can see if we pick up on anything. Otherwise, it seems pretty much a wild goose chase."

Ellie pulled her legs up under her. "I wonder how good he is as a Realtor."

"What do you mean?" Jenna got up and turned the air conditioner down.

"He says he works a lot, doesn't see his neighbors. It didn't sound like he knew the people on his street."

"Some of the houses on the street are rented in the summer. People come and go." Jenna returned to the sofa.

"I thought Realtors were outgoing, always trying to meet people." Ellie fiddled with her hair. "You know, get to know people, make contacts so they can drum up customers and sales. He doesn't seem to know many people. It doesn't seem like he puts much effort into meeting anyone."

"Maybe he's a lousy Realtor." Courtney patted Euclid's fur.

"He just recently moved back though," Jenna said. "It takes time to make friends, get to know neighbors, and settle in."

"Maybe we could take a ride over to the garage where the dad worked. Maybe there's somebody still around who knew him, though, it's a long-shot." Angie yawned.

Ellie stood up. "I'm going to get a snack and then go upstairs to read." She left the room with the cats hurrying after her.

Angie spoke in a low voice. "I'm confused about the cat's reaction to Hudson."

"How do you mean?" Jenna leaned forward. "I wasn't paying attention to them."

"You're right." Courtney nodded, thinking. "Euclid and Circe usually either hiss at people or seem to like them. They didn't seem to like Hudson, but they didn't appear to hate him either."

"I thought they seemed to be reserving judgment, like they did with Charlie Cook." Angie glanced at the doorway to be sure the felines weren't returning to the room. "I wonder why. It kind of makes me nervous."

Courtney's eyes narrowed. "The last time the cats appeared cautious with people was with those B and B guests, the Foleys, who stayed here and were involved in stealing the painting from Mr. Finch's brother."

"Maybe we better not take what Brian Hudson says to be completely true." Jenna pulled a throw blanket over her knees. "We better be on our toes around Hudson and Cook."

Courtney looked over at Angie. "When we go to Brian Hudson's house to see the garage, let's take the cats with us."

Pulses of anxiety hammered down Angie's spine. Something wasn't right. "I think that's a very good idea."

CHAPTER 15

Courtney, Jenna, and Angie pushed their way through the thicket and came out in the backyard of the Cook's house. The cats bounded across the lawn ahead of the sisters. As expected, Ellie did not want to accompany the girls on the visit to Brian Hudson's house. She remained behind to prepare the afternoon treats for the B and B guests and to tend Jenna's jewelry shop if customers came in to browse.

Hudson's tan, ranch-style house sat on a small lot next to the Cook's property. A driveway and a row of arbor vitae bushes ran between the two homes. The short driveway led to the one-car attached garage. The door was open and the girls could see that it was empty. Euclid and Circe moved slowly up the driveway with their noses to the pavement, sniffing. The orange fur on Euclid's back stood up.

Angie's heartbeat sped up. She took a deep breath to try to calm herself so that she could focus on the task ahead.

They followed the flagstone walkway to the front and just as Courtney was about to press the bell, Brian Hudson opened the door and stepped out. "Thanks for coming. Do you want to start in the garage?" He led them to the driveway and spotted Euclid and Circe sniffing around the edge of the space. Hudson's eyebrows squeezed together in a puzzled expression. "You brought the cats?"

Courtney walked past Hudson and went into the garage. "I told you, they're the ones who solved the other crimes."

Hudson gave an uneasy chuckle.

"She's kidding." Jenna pretended that what Courtney said wasn't true.

The two cats scrunched their bodies low to the ground and slinked forward two feet into the space where they stopped and sniffed a spot on the ground. Euclid raised his head and let out a piercing screech. Everyone startled. Angie could feel the thrumming in her veins.

Brian Hudson's face seemed to drain of blood and his eyes were like saucers. "How do they know?" He mumbled the words.

"Know what?" Courtney eyed the man.

"That's where the body was."

"It's just a coincidence." Angie didn't want to have Hudson freak out over what the cats could sense. She moved forward. "They're just sniffing around. They can't tell that's where your father was. It's been twenty-five years."

Euclid gave Angie a dirty look.

Angie took a quick peek at Hudson to be sure he wouldn't see her face when she glared at the orange cat for not being more discreet.

"Can you tell us what you saw that evening?" Jenna moved gingerly about the garage. She could feel an odd pulsing in her temples. *Thrum, thrum.*

Hudson ran his hand through his hair. His eyes had a wild look to them and his movements seemed more sudden and twitchy than when the girls had seen him previously. His nervous energy caused prickles to move over Angie's skin.

"I was standing there." Hudson pointed to a small landing that had two steps leading down to the garage. "That door goes to the kitchen. I came out because I heard a noise. I saw my father's car parked right there and his body was behind it, but to the right slightly." Hudson lifted his hand and angled it to demonstrate the position of the body.

Courtney and Angie walked up the steps and turned around on the landing to experience the view that Hudson had when he emerged from the kitchen that night. They imagined the crumpled body on the garage floor.

"You knew he was dead right away?" Jenna ambled around the spot where the body had fallen.

"There was a lot of blood. I was pretty sure he was dead." Hudson's words sounded hoarse.

"Then what did you do?" Jenna tried to picture the scene. She lifted her hand and rubbed her temple trying to rid herself of what seemed like the beginnings of a headache.

"I screamed." Hudson bit his lip. He didn't like admitting to the girls that he let out a cry.

Jenna continued her inquiry. "Did your mother come out then?"

Hudson stared at the spot on the floor. "Yes." The word was barely a whisper.

Circe let out a low hiss and Euclid took two menacing steps towards the man. Angie watched the felines and a chill raced through her stomach. She exchanged a look with Courtney and then asked, "What happened when your mother came out?"

"Um." Hudson stood unmoving near the spot where his father's body fell. "She ran to my father. I think she felt for a pulse, but I can't be sure. She yelled for me to call for an ambulance. I ran inside to the kitchen to place the call." He shook himself. "I remember a sense of relief that I had something to do besides stand there and stare."

"Then the ambulance came? And the police?" Courtney came off the landing and walked over to Brian Hudson. "Did they question you?"

"Of course."

"You told them what you just told us?"

Hudson nodded. "I was pretty upset. I think they gave me something to calm me down." He faced Courtney. "Funny. Some things are blocked in my memory. I can't recall some of the night."

"Were there ever any suspects?" Jenna asked.

"Not to my knowledge."

Angie left the landing. "Is there anything else you can tell us?"

"I don't think so. I think that's it." He took quick looks at the girls. "Would you like to go inside and see the letter from my mother?"

They followed Hudson into the small kitchen and he offered them seats at a round wooden table. He picked up an envelope from the counter and removed a letter written on white paper. "This is what my mother wrote to me." He placed it on the table.

Angie slid the letter over the table surface and tilted it so that she and Courtney could read it together. After reading it silently, Angie picked it up and read it aloud. She skipped the salutation and concentrated on the short paragraph. "It says, 'I couldn't part with the house even though it was full of misery. I rented it out all these years. I wish I had badgered the police to find the killer and make an arrest. I hope you can do that for me now. See if you can find the person who killed your father.'" Angie lifted her face to Hudson. "It's been so long. It will be nearly impossible to find the person responsible for your father's death. You know that, don't you?'

Hudson gave a slight nod. "I know. But I have to try."

"Can we keep this for a day or two?" Angie held

up the letter.

"Yes. I'd just like it back when you're done."

Angie nodded. "I guess that's all we can do for now. We'll head home, talk things over and decide what to do next."

***

The girls sat around the kitchen table with glasses of lemonade telling Ellie what went on during the visit to Brian Hudson's house. The cats perched in their usual spots on top of the fridge.

"The cats didn't like the garage." Jenna looked up at the two creatures. "They sensed something bad happened there." Her fingers pressed at her temple.

Angie noticed that Jenna had been pressing at the side of her face. "What's wrong? Do you have a headache?"

"I thought one was developing, but it's just this odd pulsing, sort of like a little electrical buzz. I think it's starting to fade." Jenna lifted her cold glass to the side of her head.

Ellie's eyes flicked from one sister to another.

"When did it start?" Courtney asked.

"Um, it started when we went in the garage." Jenna sat up, her eyes wide. "Oh. Was I sensing the murder?"

"I bet you were." Courtney lifted the pitcher of lemonade and refilled her glass.

"I felt the thrumming for a bit ... and prickles of worry." Angie had placed Brian Hudson's letter from his mother on the table. She glanced at it. "The letter his mother wrote must have convinced Hudson to return to Sweet Cove."

"He'd feel guilty if he didn't try to find the killer." Courtney sipped her ice cold beverage. "I got creepy sensations when we stood on the landing, but I'm not sure if it was normal feelings that anyone would have thinking of what happened in that garage or if it was something else."

Mr. Finch came into the kitchen through the back door and greeted the girls. Sweat beaded on his forehead.

"Come sit with us." Courtney stood to get another glass. "Angie made fresh squeezed lemonade."

Mr. Finch took a seat next to Angie. "I wouldn't pass up a nice cold glass of lemonade. It's so hot outside. I feared I might have a stroke walking back from the candy store."

Courtney placed the glass in front of Finch and he raised it to his lips and took a long swallow. "Delicious. You have revived me, Miss Angie."

As the sisters told him what happened in Brian Hudson's garage, Finch noticed the letter on the table and lifted the edge of the paper. "What's this?"

Jenna explained that it was a letter written to Hudson from his mother requesting he research who may have killed the father.

Finch ran his finger over the words on the paper. He looked at the girls. "His mother wrote this?"

Jenna nodded.

Finch scowled. Euclid sat up and hissed.

"What's wrong?" Courtney scrutinized Finch's face.

"No woman, besides the ones in this room, has ever touched this document."

CHAPTER 16

"What?" Courtney practically jumped from her chair.

"So it's a fake?" Jenna scowled. She reached for the letter and scanned it again. "Really? His mother didn't write this?"

Ellie frowned in disgust. "He lied to us?"

"I sense that the letter was not written by a woman." Finch took another swallow of his lemonade. "I could be wrong, of course."

"Do you get a feeling about who did write it?" Angie's eyes narrowed in anger.

Finch tilted his head. "It's definitely a masculine vibe."

"So the next question is, did Hudson write it to deceive *us* for some reason or did someone else write it to deceive Hudson?" Tiny wrinkles formed at the corners of Angie's eyes as she concentrated on who the author of the letter could be.

"And," Courtney asked, "what is the purpose for the deception? What does someone want? Is the author's purpose to actually find the murderer or is something else going on?"

"Why can't anything be simple?" Jenna groaned.

"Such deceit in Sweet Cove. Why?" Ellie wrung her hands.

Angie said, "We can add this to the list of things to solve. The bomb in the Cook family's house. Who killed Brian Hudson's father? Who really wrote this letter and why?"

"You have much to keep you occupied." Mr. Finch stood up. "I'm going to the carriage house for a shower and a change of clothes."

A look of surprise washed over Courtney's face. "You aren't going to help us?"

Finch looked back over his shoulder with a twinkle in his eye. "You know I love a good mystery. I'll be back." He opened the back door. "Don't solve it without me."

"Let's not let on to Brian Hudson that we suspect the letter is forged." Angie crossed her arms and leaned on the table.

Jenna got up to get more ice for her glass. "How could we mention it to him? We could never explain why we have suspicion that it's forged."

Courtney deadpanned. "By the way, our friend, Mr. Finch says that your mother never wrote this letter. Mr. Finch can tell just by placing his fingers on the paper." The corners of her mouth turned up imagining Hudson's reaction. "That would go over well."

The door bell rang.

"Now what?" Ellie bolted from her chair to answer the door. Her movements were always clipped and quick whenever she wanted to extract herself from a situation. This was one of those times.

A minute later, Ellie returned with Chief Martin following her into the kitchen.

"Hello, everyone." The chief greeted the girls.

"The chief wants to talk to all of us." Ellie's voice shook. "Why don't we go into the family room?"

The girls, the chief, and the cats trooped into the family room and took seats. Angie's heart thudded and some drops of perspiration traveled down her back.

"So," Chief Martin said. He sat in the easy chair near the window with his back to the rear yard. "The building inspector and the expert in explosive devices have finished with the house." He cleared his throat. "The bomb's firepower very likely would have taken out the Cook's house, Brian Hudson's house, and may well have reached even the carriage house."

Ellie had to rest against the sofa back. She took deep breaths.

"During the investigation, a discovery was made. Close to the bomb's location in the basement, in the wall, was a small, dug out crevice. Inside, we found a driver's license. It was from twenty-five years ago. It had dried blood on it. Preliminary testing indicates that the blood belongs to John Hudson, the murdered father of Brian Hudson."

Little flickers of something sparked in Angie's brain and she sat straight. "Whose license is it?"

The chief made eye contact with each girl. "It belongs to Mr. Chip Cook, the father of Charlie Cook."

"That mean, old goat is the killer?" Jenna's eyes were wide.

Angie's nervous system pinged. Her blood thrummed for several seconds. She looked at the cats. Euclid and Circe sat at attention, scowling.

"It seems so." The chief's expression was solemn.

"Wow." Courtney thought it over. "That man is a real jerk. I could picture him as a killer. But why would he kill Mr. Hudson?"

The chief placed his hands on the arms of the chair. "The 'why' is often the most puzzling in these types of cases." He let out a sigh. "Chip Cook is being brought in for questioning. He won't be arrested immediately. He may have an explanation for the license. But things don't look good for him."

"Do you think he was the one who placed the bomb in the house?" Jenna leaned forward. "To destroy evidence? Could there be other incriminating evidence in the house?"

Angie narrowed her eyes. "Why blow the place up? Why not just remove the evidence?"

"Good questions." The chief nodded. "Questions I hope we get the answers to very soon."

A wave of unease washed over Angie and she blurted. "I don't think Chip Cook is the killer."

Euclid jumped onto the coffee table, looked at Angie, and trilled.

"The cat seems to agree." Chief Martin's face was serious. "Why don't you think he did it?"

Angie was sheepish even though Euclid seemed to confirm her feelings. She had no idea why she didn't believe that Chip Cook was the killer ... she only knew that's what she felt in her blood. She shrugged one shoulder and turned her palms up.

"Okay." Chief Martin stood up. "Good to know your thoughts. Tell me if you get more information."

Ellie walked the chief to the front door and saw him out.

Courtney turned to Angie. "I think you're right about Chip Cook. We need to figure this out."

"What can we do next?" Jenna twirled a pencil between her fingers.

Angie stood up. Her shoulder muscles were tense and achy. "I need to go bake something." She headed to the kitchen with the cats at her heels.

CHAPTER 17

Flour, sugar, cinnamon, butter, and sour cream were strewn across the counter on the family side of the kitchen. In a frenzied state, Angie pulled out mixing bowls, measuring cups, a spatula, a wooden spoon, and a tube pan.

Courtney moved a stool back from the new granite topped island and sat down. "Are you going to put a spell on someone?"

Angie stopped and stared at her sister. "No." She blew out a long breath. "It's too dangerous to do that."

"Then you'd better cool down before you start mixing or there will be unintended consequences for whoever eats what you're making."

"I need to keep busy. I need to clear my head, focus on something other than the bomb and the murder. Baking helps."

"Good. I'll reap the benefits." Courtney's eyes roved over the ingredients. "What are you making?"

"Sour cream coffee cake."

Courtney smiled. "Yum. My favorite. That's what I hoped it would be." She eyed her sister. "Clear your mind of thoughts. I don't want to end up falling in love with you like Mr. Finch did after he ate what was supposed to be the 'truth' muffin."

Angie gave a sheepish smile. She still felt terrible about the "spell" she mistakenly put on Finch last month. "You're right. I'm going to think pleasant thoughts. Everything is fine. Everyone is honest and kind."

"You don't have to go that far." Courtney rolled her eyes. "Just, you know, be cheerful while you bake."

"I'll try." Angie measured out the flour and placed it in the glass bowl.

"Why don't you think old man Cook is the killer?"

"Because of the feeling I got when Chief Martin was talking to us." Angie looked across the room. "I felt thrumming. Did you?"

Courtney shook her head. "That old driver's license in the wall of the Cook's basement? Right near where the bomb was placed? I don't think so. It's a red herring."

Angie glanced up for a second. "Have you been reading mysteries?"

"No. I watch mysteries on television. A red herring is...."

Angie smiled. "I know what it is."

Jenna came into the kitchen and sat on the stool

next to her sister.

"Someone put the license there to throw us off." Courtney folded her arms and leaned on the counter. "To make us think old man Cook did it."

"But we know better." Angie added baking powder, baking soda, and salt to the flour. "Where's Ellie?"

Jenna handed sticks of butter to Angie. "She's on the sofa. She's going to take a thirty-minute nap. You think whoever placed the license in the basement is the person who planted the bomb?"

Angie put the sugar, eggs, vanilla, and butter into a bowl. She bent down to get the electric mixer from the lower cabinet. "I'm not sure. It's likely though."

"So the killer is someone who hates Cook?" Courtney tapped a finger on the counter absent-mindedly. "The killer wants to deflect attention from himself and pin the murder on Cook?"

"What came first? Did the killer murder Mr. Hudson just to pin it on Cook? Just to get Cook put in prison? Or did the murderer kill Mr. Hudson and then think to pin it on Chip Cook?" Jenna squinted her eyes, puzzling over the different possibilities.

Angie mixed together brown sugar, finely chopped pecans, and cinnamon. "If the killer's original intention was to get Chip Cook put away in jail, then why wait so long with the evidence? It's been twenty-five years. Wouldn't the killer have tried to pin the crime on Cook right away?"

Euclid jumped onto the counter.

Courtney looked at the big orange cat. "Cats should be on the floor or on top of the fridge. You can't sit on the counter."

Euclid ignored Courtney's comment. He stared at Angie and gave a low hiss which made the honey blonde baker turn and look at the huge feline.

Angie's brain prickled with something she'd overlooked. "You know, when I was at the hair salon, Gloria said something about John Hudson...." Angie's forehead scrunched in thought. "She said he was a 'rough' man." She looked at her sisters and tilted her head. "What could that mean? A bad man? Someone with no social skills? A tough guy? What?"

Jenna stood up and went to the other side of the counter. She picked up the large bowl her sister had been using and carried it to the sink. "I think another visit to the salon is in order."

"Maybe a quick visit tomorrow," Angie suggested.

"I'll go with you." Jenna filled the sink with water.

The sound of footsteps caused the girls to turn towards the doorway. Mr. Finch came into the kitchen with Betty Hayes. Finch was dressed in a suit and tie and Betty had on a long, flowing floral dress, pewter-colored sandals, and a pale blue summer cardigan.

"The kitchen looks beautiful." Betty turned in a circle in the middle of the room admiring the new layout. "You have two sides for cooking."

Courtney said, "Tom made a commercial side and a family side. There are even pocket doors so we can close the two off from one another. We aren't supposed to have cats in the commercial part of the kitchen when we're making food for the B and B or for Angie's bakery. Once it re-opens."

Euclid and Circe scowled at Courtney when she mentioned the 'no cats in the commercial kitchen' rule.

"You both look very nice," Jenna said. "Did you have dinner at the resort?"

"We had an excellent meal." Mr. Finch pulled a chair back from the kitchen table for Betty and she sat. He eased himself onto the chair next to her. "We're on our way to the carriage house for a night cap before Miss Betty returns home. We chatted at dinner about the events of the past days. We thought we might share something with you. Where is Miss Ellie?"

"She's napping." Jenna dried her hands on a dish towel. "If what you have to say has to do with the bomb, then I wouldn't wake her."

Finch looked over the tops of his glasses at his companion. "Why don't you tell them what you told me?"

Betty fidgeted in her seat. "We talked about the bomb and John Hudson's murder."

The girls and the cats listened eagerly to Betty.

"Victor...." Betty looked at Mr. Finch. "He asked me if I knew the Hudsons." She fiddled with the silver bracelets on her wrist. "I didn't really. There was scuttlebutt in town. About Mr. Hudson."

The three sisters' eyes widened with interest.

"Go on." Mr. Finch encouraged Betty.

"People talked." Betty gave a sigh. "People said John Hudson was abusive, to his wife and his son." She had a guilty expression on her face. "I never noticed anything ... well, just once. Years ago, my sister was up for a visit. She loves Bingo, though I can't stand it. I took her to the town weekly game. Mrs. Hudson was a regular there, I understand. Well, she had a black eye that night. There were bruises on her wrist. I overheard her tell someone she fell on the stairs to the basement. I didn't have any reason to doubt her story, but people whispered that it was her husband who caused the bruises." Betty's face flushed. "Time's were different back then. We didn't intrude on each other's personal affairs, unless someone asked for help." Her voice grew soft. "I guess we should have made an effort to help ... in some cases."

"So Brian Hudson's father beat him." Jenna pondered. "The man beat his wife." She made eye contact with her two sisters. "That might be motive for the wife or the son to kill him."

"This puts a new spin on things." Angie put the coffee cake in the oven.

"I thought it might be worth considering." Mr. Finch stood up and helped Betty out of her chair. "We'll head off now."

They said goodnights.

"An abusive father and husband. What a peach." Jenna scowled. "I almost want to say he deserves what he got, but I know it's wrong to think that way."

"At least the mother and son had a measure of peace after the father was killed." Courtney scratched Circe's black cheek.

"We're very lucky to have grown up in such a great family." Angie's eyes were sad. "Every child should have what we've had."

Courtney sighed. "I'm going to bed. I have an early morning at the candy store tomorrow."

"Tom's going to call in a few minutes," Jenna said. "I'll head up to my room."

Angie checked her watch. "I think I'll sit on the porch until the cake's done. It's so hot. Maybe there's a breeze out there." She and Jenna walked down the hall and into the foyer. Jenna climbed the stairs to her bedroom and Angie went out the front door to the dark porch. As she sat down in the closest rocker under the porch light, something caught her eye in the darkness a few yards away from her chair. She startled.

Charlie Cook sat in a rocking chair in the middle of the porch. "Evening."

"Oh, hi." Angie muscles tensed up and she had

the urge to run back inside the house. She tried to collect herself, but couldn't help clutching the arms of the rocking chair. "We haven't seen much of you."

Charlie looked out over the front lawn. "I've got a lot to do. I've been going home to Rye most days. It's only about a forty-minute drive when there's no traffic. I keep the room here reserved in case there's some news and I have to stay over. I know how hard it is in summer to get a room in a resort town."

"So you haven't been around here much?"

Cook shook his head. "School's out so I don't have that commitment, but I do consulting and private electrical work when I'm not teaching."

Angie wondered if Cook had heard that his father was going to be questioned in regards to John Hudson's murder. She wasn't going to mention it in case Charlie didn't know about the latest development, but she thought of asking why he had come back to Sweet Cove. "Is there any news? Is that why you came back tonight?"

"Nah. I just came back to check in with Chief Martin. See if there are any updates about the bomb. Check in with the Realtor about the house."

A flutter of unease rippled over Angie's skin. "I didn't think you had anything to do with the Willow Street house. Isn't your father the one handling the sale?"

Charlie gave a chuckle. "I guess I'm nosy."

Angie tried a different line of questioning. She glanced at the door to the house hoping the cats were sitting behind the screen door listening, but she'd closed the heavy wooden front door when she came out to the porch. "Your father doesn't involve you at all in the selling of the property?" Angie knew very well that he didn't, but she wanted to keep the conversation going.

"My father doesn't speak to me. The other day when I saw him at the house? Those few words were more than I've heard from him in the last ten years."

"Was it always like this between you?" Angie feared she was venturing into such personal territory that Charlie might get up and leave.

"Pretty much. He wasn't around a lot when I was a kid. He didn't take any interest in me. When he was home, he ignored me unless I was too noisy or bugged him in some mysterious way."

"You and your mom were close?"

"She did her own thing. She wasn't mean to me. Does that constitute close?"

"When we first met at the police station, you described your mom as being a quiet person, sort of introspective. How did she handle your dad's personality?"

"They managed. It wasn't a match made in Heaven." Charlie rocked back and forth. Angie thought his tone was too blasé. She sensed something simmering under the surface.

Ellie opened the front door and peered onto the dark porch. "Angie?"

"I'm here. Charlie Cook is here too. I'm waiting for the cake to be done. Want to come out?"

"I'm heading up to my room. I've got a slight headache. I just wanted to be sure you were okay." Ellie said goodnight to her sister and Mr. Cook.

"Leave the door open," Angie said. She hoped the cats would appear.

"You seem like you have a nice family," Cook said. "A lot different than mine."

"I'm lucky I guess. You don't have siblings? Or cousins?"

"Nope. I'm an only child. Never felt like I had a family at all. I was sent off to boarding school when I was eleven. Dad thought it would build character. Kids shouldn't be loafing around at home. It isn't easy to feel close to your parents when you're never with them." He snorted. "I didn't care. It wasn't a home I wanted to spend any time in."

Angie didn't know what to say and was saved from having to think of something to mutter when Charlie's phone buzzed. He glanced at it and stood up. "I have to take this." He wandered off the porch and across the lawn to stand on the sidewalk in front of the Victorian. Angie could hear his voice, but not the actual words. A rush of relief washed over her that their conversation was done.

As she hurried inside to check on the coffee cake, she pondered how different children's formative years could be and how they shaped the person you became. She whispered silent thanks that she grew up in a loving family.

CHAPTER 18

The heat wave broke just in time for Courtney's afternoon birthday party. The air was clear with the temperatures in the perfect mid-eighties. Josh had set aside two hotel suites at the resort for the party. The suites were side by side and each one had a full kitchen, bath, bedroom, and living room with a sliding glass door leading to a stone patio facing the ocean.

Mr. Finch and the cats had set up residence on one of the patios. A bowl of water and a dish filled with kitty kibble had been placed in the corner.

On the lawn in front of the suites, two huge picnic tables were set up, one for the buffet and one for people to sit and eat. The resort's two pools and hot tubs were just around the corner from the rooms, and the beach was only a short walk across the lawn and down a path through the sand dunes. Kayaks, tubes, and boogie boards had been placed on the beach for everyone to use.

Mr. Finch settled comfortably into one of the patio chairs to read a book and watch the goings-on. Euclid and Circe lay on a chaise lounge that was covered with soft blankets for the felines to relax on.

The sisters bustled back and forth from the cars carrying platters of food and boxes of beverages. They stocked the refrigerators in both of the suites.

"You look very comfortable sitting there, Mr. Finch." Courtney smiled at him.

"I'm very happy with my spot." Finch nodded at the chaise lounge next to him. "As are my companions." Both cats trilled. "It's lovely sitting here in the shade, relaxing, with nothing to do but watch the boats on the water and the people enjoying themselves."

The girls put out a big silver metal bin filled with ice and drinks. They put snacks on the table for people to nibble. A large glass bowl full of fruit salad was placed on top of a container of ice. Small plates and cups were set on the table along with a basket containing forks, spoons, knives, and napkins. Glass vases filled with summer flowers sat in the center of each table.

When Courtney's twenty-second birthday celebration was being planned, the sisters thought of inviting their friends from Boston, but the list became so long that they decided to keep the gathering intimate by inviting Josh Williams, Tom, Attorney Ford, Mr. Finch and Betty. An additional name was added to the list only a few days ago. Courtney was eager to include her new acquaintance, Rufus Fudge. "Acquaintance" was probably the wrong word, the sisters thought, but "boyfriend" was premature and "friend" didn't have the right feel, so, at a loss for what to call him, they gave up trying to come up with a label.

Jenna did offer a few suggestions like, "partner," "honeybun," "sweetheart," but by the time she recommended the third idea, Courtney had harrumphed out of the room.

Josh told Angie he might have to come and go throughout the afternoon and evening because the resort manager had to tend to a family situation, but he promised to spend every moment he could at the gathering. Angie spotted Josh walking across the lawn wearing swim trunks and a blue T-shirt and her muscles went so weak at the sight of him that she almost had to sit down.

Josh gave her a sweet kiss and put his arm on her shoulder as he leaned close and whispered something. Angie's eyes went wide.

"Don't tell her. It's my birthday gift to her." Josh winked.

Angie moved her index finger over her chest in the shape of an "X." "I promise not to say a word. My lips are sealed."

Josh took Angie's hand and they walked down to the beach to join Jenna and Tom in the surf. Ellie and Attorney Jack Ford were engaged in a vigorous tennis match against Courtney and Rufus.

"If you were smart," Ford told Rufus, "you'd

Sweet Deceit

make sure your employer wins this match." He stepped back to serve.

"And if you were a gentleman," Courtney said to Ford, "you'd make sure the birthday girl wins the match."

Ford chuckled at Courtney's retort and messed up his serve.

"I see you're taking my advice." Courtney flashed a smile. "Keep it up."

After the game, the four of them used the two hotel suites to change into swimsuits, and Courtney and Rufus raced one another to the beach. Ellie and Jack sat with Mr. Finch on the patio eating fruit salad and sipping sangria.

Circe surprised the attorney by jumping onto his lap and settling there.

"I never had a cat." Jack's face looked pleased as he ran his hand over the cat's ebony fur and listened to the loud purring.

"She likes you." Ellie smiled as she lifted a strawberry to her lips. "The cats are very good judges of character so you should take her acceptance as a supreme compliment."

Mr. Finch balanced his glass on the arm of his chair. "I've always loved the sound of a cat's purr. I find it very comforting."

"It is, isn't it?" Jack continued to pat the black cat and chuckled as the purring grew even louder. The sweet, gentle creature on his lap seemed to soften Ford's usual formal manner.

J.A Whiting

Mr. Finch smiled at the feline and then made eye contact with the huge orange boy sitting up on the chaise lounge, his piercing green eyes keeping watch over what was going on. Finch gave Euclid a slight nod. "There is nothing like a cat to soothe the soul."

The orange boy trilled and sat up even taller with his huge plume of a tail flowing over the side of the chair.

After conversing with Mr. Finch, Ellie and Jack decided to join the others on the beach. Jack reluctantly moved Circe to the side so he could extract himself from the chair.

Almost as soon as they were over the dunes, Betty Hayes zoomed around the corner of the building, out of breath and tapping at her phone. When she saw Mr. Finch reading in the comfort of the shade, she cooed. "Well, Victor. Aren't you the picture of contentment?"

Finch led her into the kitchen of the suite and prepared a cool drink for her. Betty wore a long lavender cotton dress that billowed around her silver sandals. Her blue eyes twinkled at the older man as he placed an orange slice on the rim of the glass. They returned to the patio hand in hand.

When the eight young people followed the path back to the resort and made their way across the lawn, they could hear Betty's girlish giggles as she sat next to Mr. Finch and flirted with him.

Tom and Josh fired up the grills and placed

152

skewers of swordfish, vegetables, and steak kabobs over the coals. The girls carried potato salad, green salad with cranberries and shaved pecorino cheese, roasted red peppers, Boston baked beans, and a medley of rice, black beans, peas, corn, and slivers of shredded carrots to the table. Jack and Rufus husked and delivered corn on the cob to Mr. Finch who prepared them in a huge pot on the stove of the suite's kitchen.

When the feast was ready, they gathered around the table and dug into the food with hearty appetites. Conversation was light and easy. As dusk fell, candles were lit and the light of the flames cast a warm glow over the friends.

Angie carried the requested birthday treat from the refrigerator to the table. Each year, Courtney wanted the same dessert, an ice cream pie with a chocolate crust and fresh fruit mixed among the filling. Twenty-two birthday candles were lit and the group burst into song wishing Courtney a very happy birthday. The birthday girl had asked that no one bring any gifts. "I have everything I need," was how Courtney explained her request.

As slices of the ice cream treat were cut, placed on glass dessert plates, and passed around, Mr. Finch announced, "I was twenty-two once."

Everyone laughed.

After the dessert was consumed and the sky darkened, Angie spread two blankets on the grass next to the patio. The young people sat down with the cats next to them. Finch and Betty were more comfortable sitting in the patio chairs.

Josh stood up. "In honor of a special someone's birthday, we've arranged a small display." He barely finished his sentence when, over the ocean, fireworks exploded in the night sky. Oohs and aahs filled the air as colorful sprays of light sparkled and spread high over the sea, courtesy of Josh Williams and the Sweet Cove Resort.

Josh snuggled next to Angie to watch the show. He took her hand, and Angie's heart swelled.

"Thank you," she whispered. "For everything."

It seemed like it had been a long time since they were all able to relax and enjoy an evening together without something picking at them to be solved.

Deep down, Angie could feel it though. It was waiting for them. Deceit ... low, sinister, and insistent.

She pushed it from her mind. She knew they would face it soon enough.

But, not tonight.

CHAPTER 19

Angie drove Jenna's car down the long, winding driveway and parked in front of the three-car garage. She hadn't seen Flora Walters for nearly two weeks and looked forward to chatting with the ninety-year-old woman. Flora was a big fan of Angie's baked goods and she had been ordering treats for home delivery since the bake shop closed for re-location. Flora's knowledge of the Sweet Cove area and its residents had been instrumental in helping the Roseland sisters solve a mystery involving their Nana. Angie looked forward to chatting for a few minutes whenever she made a delivery to the Walters' residence.

Lifting two boxes from the trunk of the car, Angie headed to the front entry way of the home and rang the bell. After a few minutes, the housekeeper opened the door. "Hello, Angie. Mrs. Walters is waiting for you. I'll bring some drinks in for both of you." The housekeeper winked. "And a plate and fork." Flora Walters had to have one of the baked items as soon as they arrived in her home.

Angie walked down the hallway and entered the conservatory to find the older woman hunched over a table, doing a pen and ink drawing.

"Oh, Angie." Flora put down her pen, and with a big smile, swiveled her chair towards the talented baker.

Angie greeted Mrs. Walters. She put the treat boxes on the coffee table. "Your drawing is beautiful." The woman was working on a picture of a small bird resting amid summer blossoms. "I didn't know you were an artist." She helped Mrs. Walters to the sofa.

"I'm not an artist, though I longed to be. When my arthritis isn't flaring up, I enjoy working with pen and ink or watercolors."

"Well, the picture is lovely."

The older woman clasped her bony hands together. "What have you brought me? Two boxes today?"

"I brought the chocolate cupcakes you requested. I made a sour cream coffee cake for my family the other day and I thought you might like one." Angie dug into her purse and retrieved a small white candy box. "I brought you some Divinity and Turkish delights from Courtney and Mr. Finch, too."

"I'm practically swooning." Flora clapped her hands with joy.

"Just don't eat it all in one day." Angie laughed.

The housekeeper brought in glasses of iced tea and she opened the bakery box and placed a cupcake on a plate. She handed it to Flora along with a fork.

"I heard you were in the house on Willow Street when that bomb was found." Flora's face pinched with concern. "I couldn't believe it. Thank heavens you weren't hurt."

Angie marveled at how word traveled through town whenever something happened.

Flora swallowed a bite of the cupcake. "I suppose there aren't any suspects yet besides Chip Cook?"

Angie's eyebrows went up. "You know about Chip Cook being questioned about John Hudson's murder?"

"When you've lived as long as I have, you make a lot of contacts." Flora looked up from her cupcake. "Of course, some can't be trusted." She speared another piece of her treat. "I assume you've met Chip Cook since someone told me they saw you at the police station."

The corners of Angie's mouth turned up thinking that Mrs. Walters would be right at home working for the FBI. "I did meet him. I was not impressed."

"Rightly so. He's a man to keep away from." Flora scowled. "Do you think the placement of the bomb and the long-ago murder of John Hudson are linked?"

Angie took a breath. "I do."

"And what do you think of the bloody license found right near the bomb?"

Angie was impressed with Flora's contacts since the older woman seemed to know everything about the case. "Courtney says it's a red herring."

"Smart girl." Flora put her plate and fork on the side table next to the sofa. "Only a fool would think Chip Cook would hide his license in the basement after murdering the neighbor." She harrumphed. "Mr. Cook has more ingenuity than that."

Angie wondered what that meant, but thought it was probably best not to know anything about the nasty Mr. Chip Cook.

Flora shook her head. "Cook didn't place the bomb and he didn't kill John Hudson. The man is guilty of plenty of crimes, but not those two acts."

Now Angie was sure she didn't want to know anything about Chip Cook. "Do you have any ideas about who is responsible, either for the bomb or the murder?"

"My thought is that when they find the killer, then they've also found the bomber, and vice versa."

"Did you know Chip Cook's wife, Elise?"

Flora made eye contact with Angie. "Somewhat. I did not approve of her behavior."

Angie understood the comment. "Did you know the Hudson family?"

"Barely. John Hudson. Another shining example of a man." Flora made a low sound of disgust in her throat. "Perhaps he got what was coming to him." The older woman had clearly heard the gossip that John Hudson had abused his wife and son.

"I talked to the son recently, Brian Hudson, he's a Realtor. He wants us to look into the murder of his father."

Flora's eyes narrowed. "Does he?" She tapped her index finger on the arm of the chair. "That's unexpected." She paused for a moment, and then continued. "I always wondered if the wife or Brian might have ... been responsible for the murder."

Angie nodded. "I wondered the same thing."

"However, why would the son ask you to look into the murder if he is the guilty party?" Flora puzzled.

"That's a good question. Brian told us that he and his mother were at home that night waiting for the dad to return from work. He said his mom was cooking dinner. Brian heard a noise in the garage, went to investigate, and found his father on the floor next to the car."

Flora leveled her eyes at Angie. "Brian Hudson said that?"

Angie nodded.

"His mother was at the Bingo hall that evening. She wasn't at home when the body was found."

Angie's mouth dropped open. "Are you sure?"

"My dear, I remember the past much better than the present. And my memory of the present is crystal clear." Flora clasped her hands in her lap. "Brian Hudson is lying about his mother being at home."

Angie's head was spinning. "Why would he lie? He must have told the police the same thing."

"The word on the street, at the time, was that Brian couldn't remember much about what happened or when it happened. He is obviously mistaken about his mother being present in the home when he found the body since I saw Mrs. Hudson at Bingo."

"Could Mrs. Hudson have killed her husband before she went to Bingo?" Angie's mind raced with questions.

"I suppose she could have."

"If she did kill him and Brian knows that she did, why would he ask us to try to solve the murder?" Angie thought about the letter that Brian said his mother wrote to him before she died asking him to investigate the crime. She decided not to mention the letter to Flora since she wouldn't be able to explain how Mr. Finch claimed it had not been written by a woman.

Flora didn't answer right away. After giving it some thought, she said, "The way I see it, there are two main scenarios."

Angie was grateful that the woman had some ideas because her own mind was a muddle.

"One, Mrs. Hudson killed her husband and went to Bingo and then Brian found the body. He doesn't know that his mother is the killer, hence he asked you to help solve the crime."

Angie pondered that and decided it was a plausible idea. She thought that Brian might have forged the letter in order to convince the sisters to look into the murder. A different possibility popped into her mind. "Here's another scenario. Brian Hudson killed his father. He inherits the house, and returns to Sweet Cove and the scene of the crime. He's worried that some day he'll be found out, so he decides to incriminate Chip Cook. Cook is a bad guy anyway so it wouldn't be out of the realm of possibility that he killed Hudson. The Cook's house is put up for sale, and since Brian is a Realtor, it would be easy for him to access the place. Maybe he found the old license in the house. Brian plants the bomb in the Cooks' house and hides the license right near the bomb so it will be discovered. He forges the letter to get us to investigate the crime because everything will point to Chip Cook."

Flora nodded. "Complicated, but very possible. It makes the most sense. Brian is trying to pin the crime on Mr. Cook."

"Except for one thing." Angie looked at Flora. "If the bomb had gone off, it would have destroyed the house and Chip Cook's license and any other evidence to be found."

Flora said, "Yes, but from what I've heard, not only would the bomb have destroyed the Cook's house, it most likely would have destroyed Brian

Hudson's house. After the bomb went off, Brian must have planned to air his suspicions that Chip Cook murdered his father and planted the bomb in order to destroy any evidence that might have remained in either house."

"That makes sense. It's possible. It's all just speculation though. We don't have any proof."

Flora had a sad expression on her face. "I guess Brian Hudson didn't care who got killed if the bomb went off. To him, it was worth the loss of life to pin the crime on Chip Cook and save his own skin."

A sickening feeling spread through Angie's body.

Flora gave the young woman a pointed look. "Be very careful around that man, my dear."

CHAPTER 20

Angie made the rest of her deliveries as fast as she could so she could get home and talk to Jenna and Ellie about Brian Hudson being the main suspect. She pulled into the Victorian's driveway and jerked the car to a halt. Hurrying up the steps to the wraparound porch, she walked to the door that led to Jenna's jewelry shop. Jenna sat at her desk working on new designs. The cats slept on the sofa against the wall.

Jenna looked up when Angie rushed into the room. "What now?"

Angie went through the entire conversation she'd had with Flora Walters.

Euclid gave a low hiss.

"That's a complicated mess of a story." Jenna crossed her arms over her chest. "But it sure makes sense. Brian Hudson kills his father because he's sick of the abuse he and his mom suffer. They move away to North Carolina. The mom dies and leaves the Sweet Cove house to Brian. He returns. He worries that he will be caught for the crime and decides to set up Chip Cook to take the fall. Interesting."

Angie sank into a chair. "We should tell Chief Martin what we think." She looked at Jenna. "We should go have another look at the garage. Now that we have a sense of what might have happened, maybe we can pick up on something."

"We need some evidence." Jenna fiddled with the gemstones on her desk for a minute and then she turned back to Angie, her eyes wide. "There must still be something in Brian Hudson's possession with his father's blood on it."

"Why?"

Jenna leaned forward. "Brian must still have some clothes item he used when he killed his father. There was blood on the old license they found near the bomb. Brian must have dug out the old shirt or whatever. He could have wet the blood stains on the clothing and then transferred some of the blood onto the license."

Angie's jaw dropped. "You're a genius."

"The evidence must be in Brian's house. Let's go see Chief Martin. Maybe they can get a warrant for a search."

Angie's face clouded. "No judge would give a warrant based solely on our speculation."

Jenna glanced out the window at the backyard. "Could we...?"

"Break in? No way."

"Not break in." Jenna faced her sister. "What if

we ask to see the garage and house again? If we wander around inside, maybe one of us could pick up on the hidden evidence."

"I can call Brian and tell him we want to look around." Angie reached for her phone.

"Let's arrange a meeting for when Courtney and Mr. Finch come home from the candy store and we'll all go together."

Angie agreed. "Safety in numbers."

***

Angie, Jenna, Courtney and Mr. Finch stood on the front porch of Brian Hudson's house waiting for him to come to the door.

"The cats were sure angry that we didn't let them come with us." Jenna pushed the doorbell a second time.

"It would be hard to explain why we brought them." Mr. Finch leaned on the porch railing. "We don't want Mr. Hudson thinking that we're eccentrics."

Courtney grinned. "I don't think being eccentric is such a bad thing."

"He's not answering." Annoyance played over Jenna's face. "Should we head home?"

Angie checked her phone for the time. "He's only a few minutes late."

To punctuate her words, the sound of a car's engine caused everyone to look to the street. Brian

Hudson pulled into the driveway as the garage door slowly rose. He drove into the bay and got out of the car.

In the waning light of the day, the four moved along the walkway to meet Hudson in front of the garage.

"Sorry I'm late. I was with a client." Hudson removed his briefcase from the back seat of the vehicle. "Where would you like to start?"

Angie spoke up. "In here, I guess." She had the same feeling of wariness that she'd felt the last time they visited the Hudson residence.

Courtney introduced Mr. Finch as a B and B boarder and the man who was looking at the Cook's house when the bomb was discovered. The two men shook hands.

Mr. Finch glanced around the garage space. "I wonder if you might back your car out. It might be helpful for us to move around in here without the car to impede our inspection."

Hudson looked surprised. He was probably wondering what the four people could possibly discover about a crime by looking at the garage twenty-five years after it happened, but he didn't say anything about it. "Sure. I'll move it into the driveway."

Once the car was out of the way, Angie and Courtney moved around inside of the dark space. The sun had set and cloud cover obscured the moon and stars. Beads of perspiration formed under

Angie's shirt from the hot, humid air. She'd always been sensitive to humidity and it felt especially oppressive in the garage from being closed up all day. She removed an elastic from her back pocket and put her hair up into a ponytail to get it off her neck.

Courtney stood on the little landing where the door led to the kitchen. She leaned forward looking around, her arms resting on the wooden railing.

"Should I turn the light on?" Hudson moved to the light switch pad on the wall.

Jenna hadn't entered the garage. She held back at the threshold. "It was dark out when the crime was committed?"

Hudson turned towards her and nodded. "It happened about this time of night. It was sort of like how it is now, almost fully dark."

"Leave the lights off then." Jenna didn't move from her spot.

Mr. Finch leaned on his cane and walked slowly around the inside perimeter of the garage. Brian Hudson stood by his car in the driveway checking his phone messages.

After a few minutes, Jenna called Brian over. "Can you go through what happened that night? I know you told us last time, but I'd like to hear it again."

Angie gave her sister a quick glance wondering why Jenna wanted Brian to explain the happenings one more time.

Brian started to tell about the evening.

Jenna held up her hand. "As you tell about it, would you go through the motions of where you stood and when?"

Hudson swallowed and shoved his hands in his pockets. "Uh, okay." He moved to where Courtney stood on the landing. He went through the motions, moving around the space explaining what he saw and what he did.

"Did you see anyone?" Jenna's eyes were glued to the spot on the floor where Hudson had indicated his father's body lay prone.

Hudson's eyes widened and Angie could see more of his eyeballs' white space in the darkened garage. "Just my father." His voice sounded shaky.

Jenna gave Hudson a piercing look, and then she flicked her eyes to the right of where she was standing. Her temples pulsed. A chill ran down her spine. She pressed her eyelids tightly shut for several seconds and then opened them. "No one? You didn't see anyone else?"

The clouds shifted in the sky and a tiny shaft of light lit Hudson's face for a moment. Jenna could see his Adam's apple move down and back up as he swallowed hard. He shook his head.

"Why don't we go inside now?" Angie suggested.

They followed Brian into the kitchen and he led the strange parade through the rooms. He returned to the kitchen for a glass of water while each of the four moved around the home at their own pace.

Mr. Finch found Hudson standing in front of the sink sipping from his glass. "Do you have your mother's will available for us to look over?"

Again, Hudson looked surprised by the request. "Sure. It's in my office. I'll get it." He walked down the hallway to the small room opposite the living room.

Angie entered the kitchen just as Hudson came in carrying a folder. He put it on the small table that was tucked into a nook. He took out the will and handed it to Finch. "Here it is."

Mr. Finch flipped the pages to the last one and he inspected Mrs. Hudson's signature. With Angie looking over his shoulder, he used his index finger to trace the lines of the woman's name. Finch handed the document back to Hudson when he'd finished his examination. "Thank you."

"What did you need to see?"

"Just checking that things are in order." Finch turned away to the living room so that Hudson wouldn't probe any further.

After fifteen more minutes of walking about the rooms, Angie asked if they might take a look at the basement. They followed the man down the stairs into a finished section of the cellar. Entering what used to be called a "rec" room was like stepping back into the 1970s with the paneled walls, a shag carpet covering the floor, and at the far end of the room, a bar with two stools in front of it and a wall decorated with sports memorabilia. Mr. Finch and the three sisters walked around the space and then checked out the storage and utility section of the basement.

When everyone was satisfied, they thanked Hudson, and left the property. The four amateur investigators walked down Willow Street in the darkness, every now and then stepping into pools of light from the street lamps. They glanced at the Cook's house when they passed it, but nobody spoke until they were a few houses away from Brian Hudson's place.

Jenna broke the silence. "He saw something that night."

"I knew you felt something." Angie held Mr. Finch's elbow so that he wouldn't stumble in the dark.

"It wasn't what I felt." Jenna hooked her arm through Courtney's. "It's what I *saw*."

CHAPTER 21

Everyone halted on the sidewalk and wheeled towards Jenna with their mouths hanging open.

"You saw something?" Excitement rippled in Courtney's voice.

Jenna rubbed her temple with her forefinger. "When I was standing near the garage, I had ... I don't know ... a vision." She made eye contact with her sisters and Finch. "Someone else was there the night of the murder. I saw the shadow of a man. He saw Brian and Brian saw him. The man turned away and ran."

"A witness?" Mr. Finch adjusted his eyeglasses. "What a very interesting development."

"Could you see his face? Anything distinctive about him?" Angie looked hopeful.

Jenna shook her head. "It was clear that it was a man, but I couldn't see his face. It was all in shadow and mostly from the back. But I know he was real. I know he was there."

"So Brian is lying when he tells us he didn't see anyone that night." Courtney sighed. "So much lying. So much deceit."

"Do you think Brian killed the witness?" Angie's words floated on a trembling breath.

"I didn't think of that possibility," Jenna whispered.

Angie turned to Mr. Finch. "What did you think about Mrs. Hudson's will?"

"The will appears genuine." Finch rested both of his hands on top of his cane. "The signature on the will and the one on the letter that we suspect is forged are different, however. The will has a more delicate signature. The point of the pen was pressed to the paper with a light touch. The letter Mr. Hudson claims is from his mother ... that signature was applied with more pressure and was written by a man. Who that man is, I cannot say."

Courtney asked, "Did anyone sense that Hudson had some evidence hidden in the house?"

Everyone shook their heads.

"The two times I've been at that house, I've felt uneasy, anxious, like something isn't right." Angie ran her hand over her hair. "But I don't get the feeling that evidence is in the house."

Jenna glanced back over her shoulder at the Hudson property shrouded in darkness. "Let's go home. I need to shower off the bad vibes." She shuddered.

They walked to the end of Willow Street and turned left on Main. In a few blocks, they were safely back at the Victorian.

***

Jenna went up to shower and Mr. Finch sat with Ellie in the living room explaining what they'd discovered from their visit to Brian Hudson's house. Euclid and Circe hissed and growled at various times during Finch's telling.

As soon as they arrived home, Rufus Fudge rang the bell and when Courtney opened the door, he greeted her with ice cream sundaes. The two sat on the front porch together eating the treats, chatting, and watching the tourists walking by on the sidewalk in front of the Victorian.

Angie was feeling exhausted. She decided to sit in the backyard for a while and decompress. Stepping out the back door of the house, she hoped there wouldn't be any B and B guests outside by the fire pit, and she breathed a sigh of relief when she saw she had the yard and gardens to herself. She sank onto one of the Adirondack chairs on the patio, leaned back and closed her eyes, grateful for the dark and silence.

When she stirred, she sensed someone nearby and jerked up.

"Have a nice nap?" Charlie Cook sat in the chair opposite her.

Angie ran her hand over her face. "What time is it?"

Charlie looked at his watch. "Looks like almost eleven." He had a bottle of beer in his hand. He lifted it to his lips and took a long draw.

"I fell asleep." Angie felt disoriented.

"I could tell."

Angie blinked a few times and yawned. "You're back from Rye, I see."

"Yup. Did you hear my dear father was questioned by the police?"

"I heard, yes. What came of it?"

"Nothing. Yet." Charlie shook his head, a look of disgust on his face. "I wouldn't be surprised if he was the killer. The idea crossed my mind a long time ago."

Angie wondered if Charlie Cook had any information that might lead to the person Jenna sensed was present in the garage the night of the killing. "Were you at home the night John Hudson was murdered?"

"I came home earlier in the evening, grabbed a bite to eat. I'd been out for the day. But I wasn't there when the hullabaloo was going on."

"You mean when the police came?"

Charlie nodded. "I'd gone out after I ate some dinner so I missed all the commotion."

"Was your dad at home?"

Charlie sighed. "I couldn't say if he was at home when it happened, but he wasn't home when I was at the house eating."

"How about your mom? Was she there?"

"She was there. I only saw her for a minute when I got home. She was up in her room. I guess she was still up there when the police arrived next door. She was usually home most of the time."

Angie felt a shiver flutter over her skin. She wanted to ask Charlie how he could see his mother so differently than others did. Elise Cook didn't sound like she was home very much due to her extracurricular activities with other men. She sure must have hid it well, if her son thought she was such a paragon of virtue.

"You left right after you ate dinner that night? Before the police arrived next door?"

"Yeah." Charlie took another pull on his beer.

"I wonder if you might have been home when the crime was being committed."

Charlie narrowed his eyes. "I never thought about that. Maybe I was."

"When you left the house after you'd had dinner," Angie asked, "did you notice anybody around?"

"There were always people around. Sweet Cove is a tourist town."

"I mean, did you notice anyone suspicious hanging around? Anyone lurking? Near your house? Near the Hudson's house? In the backyards?"

Charlie drained his beer and gave Angie a look. "Nope." He stood up and headed to the house. "Can't help you."

Angie watched him go.

Deceit. She could feel it twisting on the air.

CHAPTER 22

Angie searched around for the cats. She climbed the staircase and saw that Jenna's bedroom door was open. Her sister had on a tank top and pajama bottoms and was using a big towel to dry her long brown locks. Euclid and Circe had curled on her bed.

"There you are." Angie walked into the room.

Jenna turned. "Me or the cats?"

"Both." Angie told them about her encounter on the patio with Charlie Cook.

Jenna closed the bedroom door during the telling so no one would hear. She climbed on the bed and sat cross-legged next to the cats.

Angie said, "I know he's not telling the truth. I think Charlie saw someone that night."

Euclid stood up and arched his back.

A low growl slipped from Circe's throat.

Jenna nodded. "I think we're all in agreement with you. How can we get Charlie to reveal what he knows?"

Angie plopped on the bed. "I don't know."

They talked for another hour, and then Angie's phone buzzed with a text message. She picked it up. "It's Ellie. She says to come quick. She's in Mr. Finch's apartment. They want us to see something."

Jenna whipped off her pajama bottoms and slipped into jeans. "Let's go."

The two sisters and the two cats tore out of the bedroom, down the stairs, out the back door to the carriage house and up to Mr. Finch's apartment. His door was ajar.

Jenna pushed the door open. "Are you here?'

Ellie called. "We're in the spare bedroom."

When the girls and the cats reached the threshold of the darkened room, they saw Ellie standing by the window a little to one side and Mr. Finch sitting in one of the kitchen chairs that they'd carried into the room and placed near the window.

"Ellie walked me home." Mr. Finch waved for the sisters to come into the room. "She came in here to shut the windows for me."

"I saw something fishy in Brian Hudson's back yard." Ellie didn't turn around, but kept looking out at the neighbor's property. "We've been sitting here doing surveillance."

Euclid jumped up onto the wide windowsill. Circe perched on the bed behind the observers.

Angie stepped closer and leaned down to peer out over the orange cat's head. "What did you see?"

"Someone walking around the back of the house

with a flashlight." Ellie kept her voice low as if the person in the next yard might be able to hear.

"But we haven't seen him for a few minutes." Finch pushed his chair back so Jenna could take a look.

"What do you make of it?" Jenna couldn't see anything in the dark yard.

"It could just be Brian Hudson walking around his place." Ellie stood up and stretched. "Maybe he heard a noise and came out to see what it was." She sat on the bed next to Circe.

Jenna eyed Angie. "Maybe we should go take a look?"

Angie nodded.

"No." Ellie almost shouted. "Do not go over there."

"We'll just peer through the bushes. See if we can see anything." Jenna headed out of the room.

Angie looked at Ellie. "If we aren't back in twenty minutes or you don't get a text from us in that time ... call Chief Martin."

Euclid let out a long hiss. He leaped off the windowsill and raced to follow Jenna.

"No cats." Angie hurried after them. "Euclid and Circe need to stay here. I don't want them hissing and giving away our position."

Jenna looked from the cats to her sister. "Are you sure? They come in handy a lot."

Angie considered for a few moments. "Oh, all right, but you two need to be as quiet as a...." She started to say "mouse" but stopped in mid-sentence thinking the felines would be insulted by being compared to a mouse. "As quiet as the grave."

Jenna made a face as she opened the apartment door. "Grave? Not a good choice of words."

The four of them ran down the stairs and through the back yard to the tree line.

***

"Can you see anything?" Jenna knelt in the bushes straining to see past the branches and leaves.

"Nothing," Angie whispered. "Wait, I think the garage door is open."

Jenna stood up quietly and pushed aside a tree branch. She held it so her sister could walk past. They moved slowly closer to the edge of Brian Hudson's property.

When they were nearly out of the camouflage of the trees, Jenna pulled on Angie's arm. She pointed to the open garage and leaned close to her sister's ear. "Someone's next to the car, lying on the floor. I can see the outline of the body in shadow."

The girls looked around for anyone else lurking in the yard. They hunched over and inched across the grass and onto the driveway until they were just a few feet from the garage.

"It's Brian Hudson." Jenna rushed forward. "There's blood."

Angie looked all around the yard as she hurried forward.

Blood flowed from a gash on Hudson's head. His briefcase lay next to him. Jenna knelt next to the man and reached for his neck to feel for a pulse. "He's alive."

Angie grabbed for her phone from her back pocket to call for an ambulance. Just as she lifted it from her jeans, it was smacked from her hand and a blow to her shoulder sent her careening forward and crashing to the cement floor. Her arms extended to cushion her fall and her hands skidded over the rough garage floor.

Jenna gasped and wheeled around on her knees.

A figure loomed over them. "Looking for someone?" Charlie Cook held a baseball bat in his hands. "Get up. Carry Hudson inside. Move."

Angie crawled over, stood up, and took hold of Brian Hudson's arms while Jenna lifted his legs. They shuffled along and managed to pull him up the few stairs of the landing and into the kitchen where they lay him down on the ceramic tiles.

On the floor, next to the refrigerator, was a bomb.

CHAPTER 23

"You." Angie sneered.

Charlie eyed her. "I'm not really sure you're in a position to be indignant." He yanked two kitchen chairs away from the table and placed one on each side of the room. "Take your seats, ladies."

Angie looked at the bomb. It didn't seem to be set. Yet.

"Why are you dong this?" Angie demanded. Her heart thundered and her head buzzed and she felt like the room was spinning in slow motion. She wanted to get Charlie talking so that time would pass and Ellie would make the emergency call to the police as they'd planned if the sisters hadn't contacted her in twenty minutes. Angie wondered how much time had already passed. "You killed John Hudson."

Brian Hudson moaned.

"You should have figured it out before now." Charlie grabbed some rope from the top of the table. "Guess you're not very good criminal justice consultants, are you?"

"Why did you kill him?" Angie took a few steps to stand behind the chair on the left side of the kitchen. She made eye contact with Jenna who stood next to the other chair.

Charlie cut the length of rope into three pieces. When he looked at Angie, his face was hard. "My sweet mother was having an affair with Mr. John Hudson. Just another loser in a long list of men my mother ... got to know. Her behavior destroyed our family. It was the last straw. With the neighbor? Right under our noses? Right in our faces. I decided, no more." Charlie tied the unconscious Brian Hudson's hands behind his back. "I saw Mr. Hudson come home. I got my bat. I went outside and waited until he got out of the car."

"You killed him ... because of your mother?" Jenna's words left her throat in a hiss.

"Yup. And old Brian here saw me. He came into the garage from the kitchen and stared right at me. I told him if he told anyone, then he'd follow in his father's footsteps." Charlie moved towards Angie with a length of rope. "Turn around. Give me your hands."

Angie started to turn, but then she grabbed the chair and lunged at Charlie. Jenna did the same, and the chairs crashed against the man's head.

An orange flash and an ebony gleam blazed through the air and landed on Charlie's back just as Courtney and Rufus Fudge dashed into the room.

Charlie leaped up screaming, with the cats

clinging to him. Rufus picked up the baseball bat and swung it at Charlie's legs. The criminal went down with a thud.

The wail of a police car could be heard approaching.

Angie, still holding the chair and sucking in air, wheezed to Rufus. "How does an Englishman know how to swing a bat?"

Rufus, brandishing the bat at the howling Charlie Cook, winked. "My mother is American. She loves baseball."

***

Almost everyone ended up at the emergency department of the nearby hospital. Chief Martin wanted to question the participants as soon as possible and Charlie Cook, Brian Hudson, and Angie needed medical attention. Angie had an x-ray done on her shoulder which indicated nothing broken so the doctor gave her a prescription for a mild pain killer. The doc warned that her shoulder and neck would be extremely sore for a few days and encouraged her to rest.

Brian Hudson had a concussion and would stay overnight for observation. Charlie Cook had cuts and bruises on his face, head, and back from Angie and Jenna pummeling him with the chairs and the cats attacking him. Cook had large purple bruises forming on the back of his legs where the baseball bat hit him, but there were no fractures.

"I didn't hit him very hard," Rufus reported. "But if he got back up ... well, that would have been another story."

Ellie and Mr. Finch collected the brave and determined felines and brought them home for a reward of tuna and much cheek scratching.

Chief Martin found the weary group sprawled in chairs in a hospital waiting area. Angie and Jenna had dark circles under their eyes and were slumped over, dozing. Courtney and Rufus had taken turns fetching bottles of water and hot tea and keeping an eye on the twin sisters while they snoozed in the uncomfortable chairs.

The girls roused, rubbing their eyes, when the chief took a seat across from them.

"Thanks for waiting to talk with me." The chief's facial muscles sagged from fatigue. "Charlie Cook has confessed to the twenty-five-year-old murder of John Hudson. He also confessed to threatening Brian Hudson to keep quiet or he'd be dead, too."

"He was only fourteen at the time. He must have been terrified of Charlie," Jenna noted.

"In fact, Brian Hudson revealed that he was still living in fear of Cook. It seems Cook paid Brian several recent nighttime visits threatening him to keep quiet."

"That must have been what he was doing when I saw him skulking around in the Willow Street backyards with a flashlight late at night." Angie's lips were tight and thin.

The chief continued. "Brian Hudson also revealed that he felt huge relief when his father died. He is full of guilt for feeling that way, but it's understandable since it ended his and his mother's torment from the man."

Courtney shook her head. "So much lying. Elise Cook and her affairs. Who knows what crimes that horrible Chip Cook has committed ... and the way he treated his son was inexcusable. No wonder Charlie Cook turned out as he has with those two as his parents."

"So Charlie Cook put the bomb in his parents' house?" Jenna asked. "But why? What was he trying to accomplish?"

Chief Martin couldn't suppress a yawn. "Cook had hidden evidence in the basement of his parents' place. He learned they were selling the house and he worried the evidence might be discovered. Then he found out Brian Hudson was back in Sweet Cove living in his family home. Charlie was concerned that Brian wouldn't keep quiet about the night of the murder. He decided to destroy his parents' house. The placement of the bomb would have damaged or destroyed Brian's house as well. Charlie wanted Brian out of the picture. And he reported that if his own father happened to die from the house bomb, it would be an added benefit." The chief let out a long sigh. "If by chance, Brian wasn't killed in the house explosion,

Charlie had other plans to take him out."

"What about the bloody license in the wall by the bomb?" Jenna questioned.

"Charlie hid the clothes he'd worn when he killed John Hudson in the Willow Street house. He'd found his father's license in the house years ago. Charlie put some water on the old blood stains from his shirt and rubbed it on the license. He hoped the license would incriminate his father, but that was only a side benefit. He really wanted to destroy the house and the evidence hidden inside it. His second goal was to kill Brian Hudson."

"What about the letter Brian claimed his mother wrote urging him to investigate the murder of his father?" Angie asked.

The chief's eyebrows went up. "Brian forged it. He wanted to convince you girls to investigate hoping that you'd discover Charlie was the murderer. Then Brian could rest easy without always wondering when Charlie would come after him. He thought a letter from his mother would pull at your heart strings."

"It did," Jenna said. "Until we found out it was a forgery."

Rufus turned to Jenna. "How did you discover the letter was forged?"

Jenna had forgotten that Rufus didn't know about people's powers. She wasn't sure how to answer his question and was thankful when Courtney replied to him. There was no way anyone could reasonably explain Mr. Finch's ability to the young Englishman, so Courtney deflected Rufus' interest by squeezing his hand and saying, "It's a long story. I'll tell you another time."

"That's the gist of the evening's discoveries." Chief Martin leaned forward in his chair. "I suggest everyone head home and get some rest." He made eye contact with each person in the room. "Thanks to all of you ... for everything." The chief got up and took a deep breath.

The others stood and stretched. They threw out the many empty paper cups that they'd accumulated, gathered their things, and headed for the door.

Courtney had borrowed Ellie's van to cart her sisters and Rufus to the hospital and back home again.

As they filed out into the hallway, Chief Martin leaned close to Angie, cleared his throat, and whispered. "Thank the cats for me, would you?"

Angie gave him a smile and nodded.

Courtney drove the van along the quiet, dark streets of Sweet Cove with Rufus in the front passenger seat and Jenna and Angie nodding off in the back. She turned the vehicle into the Victorian's driveway, the warm glow of the porch light like a beacon welcoming them home.

CHAPTER 24

The next morning, Ellie and Mr. Finch clucked over Angie and Jenna who were eating their breakfast sitting in the chairs on the patio. Euclid and Circe sat on the chaise lounge across from the girls soaking up the sun.

Ellie cooked her sisters their favorite breakfast items and Mr. Finch brought out his battery-powered heating pad and gently placed it against Angie's shoulder and neck. Her injury was so stiff that she walked around without moving her head and with her shoulder contracted nearly to her ear which made her resemble Frankenstein or some other monster.

"I didn't think this shoulder thing was going to be so uncomfortable." Angie winced when she reached for her tea cup.

Courtney emerged from the back door in her pajamas. "I think Angie is milking this in order to get waited on." She smiled at her sister and sat down next to her.

"I assure you I would not wish this on anyone."

Angie reconsidered. "Except maybe Charlie Cook."

Courtney spied the plate of eggs and bacon on Jenna's lap. "Is there any for me?"

"You have to make your own breakfast." Ellie refilled Jenna's coffee.

"May I remind you," Courtney said. "That I was also involved in the rescue efforts for my sisters."

Ellie rolled her eyes, but couldn't help but smile. "I'll get you a plate of food. I'd forgotten you were a hero, too." She headed inside to retrieve some breakfast for Courtney. Ellie looked back over her shoulder. "You know, if you keep solving crimes and helping save people from danger, Chief Martin just might have to give you that shiny deputy's badge you've been pining after."

Courtney beamed at the idea.

She and Finch had pre-arranged to have the morning off from the candy shop. It was lucky planning since the entourage didn't get back from the hospital until after three in the morning and Ellie, Mr. Finch, and the cats stayed up to greet the brave young people as they stumbled sleepy and bleary-eyed into the house.

Angie looked at Courtney. "So you and Rufus found out we were in Hudson's house from Ellie and Mr. Finch?"

"No one was at home. We looked around and couldn't find any of you. I texted Ellie. She called me and told me what was going on. Rufus and I hurried over to Hudson's house just as you carried

Brian from the garage to the kitchen. We snuck into the garage, found the cats there, and waited for the right moment to rush in." Courtney beamed. "We did a good job."

"You certainly did." Jenna smiled.

Mr. Finch took a seat in the chair next to the chaise lounge. He reached over and scratched Circe's and Euclid's cheeks. "Such fine creatures."

The cats puffed up at the praise.

"Oh," Angie said. "I almost forgot." She looked at the two fine felines. "Chief Martin thanks you for your assistance."

Euclid trilled.

"Their heads are going to swell from all this praise." Jenna scooped the last bite of her eggs into her mouth.

"It is well-deserved." Mr. Finch nodded to the cats and then to the three sisters sitting across from him. "Despite our run-ins with the criminal element, I remain optimistic about the world as I am surrounded by remarkable beings."

Angie smiled at Mr. Finch.

Ellie came out of the house with Courtney's breakfast.

Mr. Finch said, "I have something to discuss with all of you." Eyes turned towards the older man. "It's about the Willow Street house. I am considering making an offer on it and I would like your opinion."

"Isn't it full of ... bad karma?" Ellie shivered.

"I thought about that, and I wondered if perhaps, I could reverse the negative energy and fill the place with calm and contentment."

"You know you're welcome to live in the carriage house forever." Courtney licked her fork.

Mr. Finch laughed. "Forever is a long time, Miss Courtney."

"If you have to move out," Angie said, "it would be wonderful to have you right there behind the trees."

"That's what I was thinking." Finch turned and pointed to the edge of the yard. "What if we removed some of that brush right over there? Then I could have a stone mason put in a walkway from my back yard to yours. I thought that a couple of old-fashioned lamplights could be installed along the stone walk to light the way."

"How lovely." Ellie smiled at the idea.

"I bet you can get that house with a very low offer." Courtney finished her breakfast. "After all the stuff that's gone on in there, no one else would ever want it."

Finch nodded. "My thought exactly." His face took on a worried expression. "You won't be afraid to visit me there will you?"

"Try and keep us away," Jenna warned.

Circe jumped onto Finch's lap and settled, purring. The big orange boy sat up and trilled at Finch.

"I'll talk to Miss Betty about it later today."

Angie's phone buzzed and Courtney handed it to her so she wouldn't have to stretch and hurt her neck.

"It's Josh." Angie pushed herself out of her seat with a groan. She walked slowly towards the front of the house so she could talk in private.

"I still don't understand why you girls have to move away from us when you get a call from your beaus." Mr. Finch's eyes twinkled.

"You know very well why we move away." Courtney put her feet up on Angie's vacated chair and tilted her face towards the sun. "Maybe we should let our employees run the candy shop every day and we can just sit around and relax."

"After a day of relaxation, you'd be itching for something to do." Ellie collected the empty plates.

Angie shuffled back to her chair and eased into sitting position. "Josh has an offer for us."

The three sisters, Finch, and the cats looked eagerly at Angie.

"There's a huge wedding that's going to be held at the resort. It's all very last minute. He said there will be at least three hundred people attending."

"Who on earth is having such a huge event?' Ellie asked.

"It's the daughter of a Senator. A very wealthy family. Josh is anxious to have everything go well. He's asked me to make the wedding cake." She looked at Courtney and Finch. "And he'd like to have gift bags made up with candy from your confectioner shop." Angie turned to Jenna. "He would also like you to supply jewelry items for the gift bags and possibly do necklaces and earrings for the wedding party. The bride is going to contact you." She looked at Ellie. "He's asked me to check with you to see if you have any free nights available at the B and B. Since everything is so last minute, he's worried that there won't be any rooms in Sweet Cove for the guests attending the event."

Ellie nodded. "I'll check."

"And," Angie said to Ellie, "Josh would like to know if you might be able to act as wedding consultant to the bride. He knows how great your organizational skills are. He wants to talk to you about it soon."

Ellie's eyes widened in surprise. "How interesting."

"So much for relaxing." Courtney chuckled. "This is going to be fun."

"For once, at least, our efforts won't involve a mystery." Mr. Finch scratched Circe's cheek.

Angie glanced around at her companions and smiled to herself. She hoped that Mr. Finch's statement was true, but she guessed that it wouldn't be long before a new mystery would descend on them demanding to be solved. Until then, she was going to nurse her sore shoulder by sitting in the sun, in the care of her loving family.

THANK YOU FOR READING!

BOOKS BY J.A. WHITING CAN BE
FOUND HERE:

www.amazon.com/author/jawhiting

To hear about new books and book
sales, please sign up for my mailing list
at:

www.jawhitingbooks.com

Your email will never be sold, shared, or
spammed.

COZY MYSTERIES

The Sweet Dreams Bake Shop (Sweet Cove Cozy
Mystery Book 1)
Murder So Sweet (Sweet Cove Cozy Mystery Book
2)
Sweet Secrets (Sweet Cove Cozy Mystery Book 3)
Sweet Deceit (Sweet Cove Cozy Mystery Book 4)

And more to come!

MYSTERIES

The Killings (Olivia Miller Mystery - Prequel)
Red Julie (Olivia Miller Mystery - Book 1)
The Stone of Sadness (Olivia Miller Mystery - Book 2)
Justice (Olivia Miller Mystery - Book 3) Late Summer 2015
Summoning the Earth (Olivia Miller Mystery - Book 4) Late Fall 2015

J.A Whiting

If you enjoyed the book, please consider leaving a review.

A few words are all that's needed.

It would be very much appreciated.

ABOUT THE AUTHOR

J.A. Whiting lives with her family in New England where she works full time in education. Whiting loves reading and writing mystery, suspense and thriller stories.

VISIT ME AT:

www.jawhitingbooks.com

www.facebook.com/jawhitingauthor

www.amazon.com/author/jawhiting

SOME RECIPES FROM
SWEET DECEIT

ANGIE'S SOUR CREAM COFFEE CAKE

Ingredients For The Cake

*1 stick unsalted butter (at room temperature)
*1 cup sugar
*2 large eggs
*1 teaspoon vanilla extract
*2¼ cups unbleached All-Purpose Flour or cake flour
*1½ teaspoon baking powder
*¼ teaspoon baking soda
*½ teaspoon salt
*1 cup (8 ounces) sour cream or yogurt
*You may use low-fat (NOT nonfat) sour cream or yogurt (use plain or vanilla)

Ingredients For The Topping

*½ cup light brown sugar (packed)
*¼ cup of all-purpose flour

*2 teaspoons ground cinnamon
*2 teaspoons vanilla
*2-3 Tablespoons unsalted butter
*½ cup (2 ounces) chopped walnuts, optional

Directions

*Preheat the oven to 350 degrees.

*Grease and flour a 9 or 10 inch tube pan.

*Cream together the butter, sugar, eggs, and vanilla.

*In a separate bowl, mix together the flour, baking powder, baking soda and salt.

*Add the flour mixture to the butter mixture and alternate with the sour cream or yogurt. Stir in between each addition.

*For the topping, in a separate bowl, mix together brown sugar, flour, cinnamon, vanilla, and butter (and nuts if you are using them) – works best if you use your fingers to combine the ingredients into a crumbly mixture.

*Spread half the batter in the pan, and sprinkle with half the topping mixture.

*Repeat with remaining half of batter and topping.

*Bake the coffeecake in a preheated 350°F oven for 50 to 60 minutes, or until a toothpick or cake tester comes out clean.

*Cool it for 10 to 15 minutes, and then remove from the pan.

FINCH AND ROSELAND'S TURKISH DELIGHTS

Ingredients

*3 envelopes unflavored gelatin
*3 cups sugar
*⅛ teaspoon salt
*2¼ cups water
*1 Tablespoon Rose water
*2 Tablespoons of lemon juice or orange juice
*1 teaspoon of grated lemon rind or orange rind
*Drops of food coloring (optional)
*1 cup powdered sugar

Directions

*Mix gelatin, sugar and salt in a sauce pot.

*Add water.

*Bring to slow boil and then gently simmer (do not stir) for 10 minutes.

*Remove from heat and stir in your choice of juice and the rind.

*Add a few drops of food coloring (if desired).

*Taste for flavor; you can add more juice to preference.

*Pour the mixture into 8 inch square pan which has been rinsed in cold water – better if the pan is wet when you pour in the mixture.

*Chill overnight.

*Cut into squares and gently roll each square in powdered sugar.

COURTNEY'S BIRTHDAY FRUIT AND ICE CREAM TREAT

Ingredients For The Crust

*1 cup graham cracker crumbs
*1 cup chocolate wafer crumbs
*5 Tbs. unsalted butter, melted
*⅓ cup sugar
*¼ cup of shaved semi-sweet or dark chocolate

Ingredients For The Ice Cream

*3 cups vanilla or reduced-fat vanilla ice cream, softened
*1¼ cups of cut up (bite-sized) fruit – strawberries, blueberries, pitted cherries – use your choice of fruit or combine different types
*Set aside about ¼ cup of fruit to use as a garnish
*2 tablespoons mini chocolate chips (optional)

Directions For The Crust

*Preheat the oven to 350°F.

*In a bowl, combine the graham cracker crumbs and the chocolate wafer crumbs, butter and sugar and stir until the crumbs are well moistened.

*Pat the mixture firmly and evenly along the bottom and all the way up the sides of a 9-inch pie pan.

*Bake until the crust is firm, about 5 minutes. For a firmer, crunchier crust, bake for 5 minutes more.

*Remove from the oven.

*Sprinkle the crust with the shaved chocolate – it should melt into the warm crust (this step is optional).

*Let cool completely.

*Makes one 9-inch crust.

Directions For The Ice Cream Filling

*Gently combine the softened ice cream and 1 cup of the cut-up fruit in a large bowl.

*Transfer to the crust and garnish with the remaining ¼ cup of cut-up fruit and chocolate chips (if desired).

*Freeze until firm, at least 4 hours.

ANGIE'S FRUIT AND CREAM CHEESE
DANISH
(THE EASY WAY)

Ingredients

*8 ounces cream cheese
*½ cup sugar
*1 teaspoon vanilla extract
*3 Tablespoons all-purpose flour
*1 cup fruit (blackberries, blueberries, strawberries)

Ingredients For The Icing

*½ cup powdered sugar
*2 Tablespoons heavy cream
*⅛ teaspoon vanilla extract

Directions

*Thaw puff pastry in refrigerator overnight.

*Unfold pastry and place on lightly floured surface. Puff pastry comes folded in 3rds, so cut in thirds both ways, giving you 9 mini Danish.

*Preheat oven to 375 degrees.

*In a small bowl, combine cream cheese, sugar, flour and vanilla.

*Carefully spread cream cheese filling 2-3 inches wide down the center of each piece of dough.

*Top with fresh fruit of your choice.

*Fold dough pieces up over filling, alternating sides.

*Bake for 20-30 minutes or until filling is set and dough is golden in color.

*Cool before removing from baking sheet.

*In a small bowl, mix together powdered sugar, vanilla and heavy cream to create icing. You may need to add more cream to get the desired consistency.

*Drizzle icing over the Danish.

*Serve.

Made in United States
North Haven, CT
17 December 2022